LEA

Everyon Webster practical of young ladies. No dilemma was too difficult for her to solve, no emergency was too perilous for her to cope with. But now a proud princess of the realm was being held captive in a den of thieves.

And the handsome lord who could never be more than a friend was being held hostage to his own folly.

Desperately, both of them turned to her for help.

For the first time in her levelheaded life Elizabeth found herself in over her head in romance and intrigue—as she had to deal with scandal in the highest of places and a love that was hidden in the most secret depths of her own yearning heart. . . .

The Runaway Princess

by
Caroline Brooks

A SIGNET BOOK

NEW AMERICAN LIBRARY

This one's for Bill Kirby, with thanks

Copyright © 1987 by Caroline Brooks

SIGNET TRADEMARK REG. U.S. PAT. OFF. AND FOREIGN COUNTRIES
REGISTERED TRADEMARK—MARCA REGISTRADA
HECHO EN CHICAGO, U.S.A.

SIGNET, SIGNET CLASSIC, MENTOR, ONYX, PLUME, MERIDIAN
and NAL BOOKS are published by NAL PENGUIN INC.,
1633 Broadway, New York, New York 10019

First Printing, April, 1987

1   2   3   4   5   6   7   8   9

PRINTED IN THE UNITED STATES OF AMERICA

1

A misty autumn shower had occupied the whole of the morning hours, but just after noon-time, the gray clouds lifted, to be replaced by a warming and golden sunlight so pleasant that the French doors leading from the back parlor of the rectory had been opened to allow warmth and light to enter the room, thereby illuminating the single occupant, a young woman of some twenty-odd summers, dressed in a simple round gown of bottle green, her fair head bent over a piece of needlework in her lap as her busy fingers plied a needle in and out of the fabric. Her hair was plainly dressed, the sandals that peeked out beneath the single flounce on her hem were sturdy rather than fashionable, and her only ornament was a gold turnip watch fastened to her bodice, to which she glanced from time to time, betraying a slight air of boredom. Fridays at the rectory were, by long custom, the days upon which the rector himself was locked away in his study across the hall, where he engaged in the task of making up his sermon for the coming Sunday services, and from time to time the peace of the house was disturbed by a muffled exclamation or a sonorous phrase uttered in the histrionic tones of a Kean; but not even the hunting dogs drowsing at the young woman's feet stirred, so much was this behavior a part of the routine of the house. The only other sound that penetrated the peace of the afternoon was that of the washerwoman turning the mangle in the kitchen garden to the rear of the rectory. In another week, the threshers would begin their work of harvesting the glebe fields, and then all would be chaos and white-smocked threshers tromping about wanting vast platters of food and kegs of good Devonishire ale; but today there was only a drowsy quietude that should come with a well-managed household. In the spirit of the season, as well as the current political climate, the rector had chosen Proverbs 11:26 as his text, and the young lady barely listened as his gravelly voice tried first this phrase, then that, about withholding corn.

Miss Elizabeth Webster was not a beauty, but there was a pleasantly attractive air about her regular features and graceful form that

prevented even her sternest critics from label-
ing her a *jolie-laide*, and she frequently be-
moaned a countenance so open and so much
the mirror of her nature that it was hard for
her not to betray, at the worst possible times, a
sadly deplorable sense of levity such as should
not be found in the daughter of a rector—but
it was this very humor that gave her a light-
ness and charm that might save an otherwise
rather severe face. In her later years, she would
be called "handsome," and had she but known,
this very handsomeness of blue eyes and fine,
broad bone structure would stand her looks in
better stead than those of her contemporaries
who had been called "diamonds of the first
water" in their youth. Try as she might to
believe that beauty was not as important as a
pure soul and a modest heart, Miss Webster
was female enough to feel just a *little* envious
of someone like, perhaps, Lady Serene Ramplesham, one of those very diamonds of the first
water who had taken London by storm in the
Season they had shared.

"So, I say unto you, my brethren, if a man
shall *not* sell his corn, what shall he do?" the
rector's voice boomed out, and Elizabeth sighed
in sympathy for her poor papa. He was univer-
sally known as the Sporting Rector, and she
was fairly certain that the lure of the trout
stream was placing a heavy temptation upon
his good-natured soul on such a day as this,

when all he had to do was glance out his window to fairly see the big fish breaking water and sparkling in the sunlight down the meadow past the church.

"Hullo, old girl! I say, what's keeping you indoors on a fine afternoon such as this?" cried a familiar voice, and Elizabeth looked up from her needle more in relief than surprise, for nothing could have been less startling than the entrance of a gentleman in a canvas fishing jacket and oiled breeches, stepping over the window with his rod and creel in hand.

"I pray you, George," she said immediately as she rose to greet him, "do not allow Papa to see you so attired, or you shall break his heart entirely! It is *Friday!*"

No further explanation was required for George Worthington, Lord Ventor, as he propped his rod against the wall and laid his creel upon the floor at his feet. He was a sturdy-looking man in his mid-twenties, with a broad, clean-shaven face and a swarthy complexion, somewhat reddened by exposure to the sun. There was a decidedly military bearing to his posture and dress, proclaiming him to have been a soldier during the late wars, and indeed he still might have been Colonel Ventor of the Twenty-ninth had not his elder brother succumbed to the influenza some four years previously, leaving neither wife nor issue.

"Of course I know it's Friday, Lizzie," George

said a little impatiently, casting himself into the chair opposite her own and regarding her with a grin of even white teeth as he selected an apple from the dish on the table between them and bit into it with relish. "That's why I'm here!"

From the circumstance of having been brought up together from the time they were still in the charge of their wet nurses, Miss Webster and the viscount stood upon very little ceremony with one another, and seeing that there was no need to disturb Appledore with a request for the Madeira, Miss Webster settled back in her chair and picked up her needlework again.

"Catch you busy, Lizzie?" George asked, swallowing his apple.

She shook her head. "Just some charity shirts, and dull work they are, too," she added quite honestly, casting the linsey-woolsey aside, regarding George with her head to one side. "I do hope you've brought me some fish for supper, because otherwise I'm afraid we're in for some of Mrs. Gaskill's mutton stew, if you care to stay."

"Well, I don't think I can stay all that long," George said, resting a foot upon the fender of the empty grate and propping his square chin in his hand.

Elizabeth repressed a smile. "Then I suppose you had better tell me what it is you've come about, George. Not in the suds, are you?"

George's eyebrow shot upward. "For a parson's daughter, Lizzie, I don't know where you pick up some of your language," he said.

"From you, of course," Elizabeth replied without turning a hair. "Now, do not keep me in suspense a moment longer, if you please! Have you come to tell me that you've pulled the Hall out of the River Tick at last?"

"You're a right'un, Lizzie, and no mistake! I was over the fields this morning with my bailiff, and it would seem as if this might be the year that we can finally say that Ventor Hall is back upon its feet again, all right and tight!"

Elizabeth's smile was genuine. "That is good news, George! You have certainly worked hard enough to bring it all about."

George nodded thoughtfully. "Considering that I'm neither brought up nor bred for estate management, and that m'father and brother between them did all they could to wring every last groat out of the land without putting so much as a shilling back in, I do think that Morgan and I have pulled it off at last," he said, referring to his bailiff. He grinned. "And so we had a glass to it at lunch this noon, too, I don't mind tellin' you! I celebrated by taking the rest of the afternoon off and going fishing. However, that don't signify right now—well, it

10

does, but it's not what I came to talk to you about."

Elizabeth felt a delicate flush creeping into her cheeks. This moment was not quite unexpected, after all. "Thing of it is, Lizzie, since Fred took a header and I came back from Spain, time and time again I've had to seek your advice out on one thing or another. I wasn't bred to be the lord, much less to know the first thing about farming, and you've always helped me right and tight, like a good friend should."

"I try," Elizabeth replied modestly. "After all, Papa certainly has left the care of the glebe mostly to my management since Mama died, and one does learn, you know, how things ought to be done."

George, who had been absentmindedly stroking the belly of one of the rector's hunting dogs, now rose from his chair, and clasping his hands behind his back, began to pace the length of the Turkey carpet in the parlor. While Elizabeth sat with her hands folded quietly in her lap and regarded his back, George cleared his throat a number of times before finally turning to face her. "Well, Lizzie, it's rather like this. Now that I've put the Hall back into the black again, and things look as if they're pulled up right and tight, it's time to think about doing my, er, well, my duty to the family. *You* know." He cleared his throat violently. "You know, marry. Produce an heir and all of that."

Miss Webster expressed emotion by raising her eyebrows slightly. If the hands that picked up the shirt and began to lay in stitches again shook slightly, George was far too preoccupied to notice.

His face was crimson beneath his tan. "Well, you know, it's like this, Lizzie. I've come to seek out your advice once again. I've found the lady, but I don't know how to ask her."

Elizabeth's glance dropped to her needlework, a faint flush appearing in her cheeks. "I should suppose that it would only be necessary to ask her father if you might pay your addresses. The lady, of course, should have given you some indication that your suit is acceptable to her, you know."

"Well, then, yes, I suppose that is how it's done!" George exclaimed. "But dash it, Lizzie, the idea of facing Lord Ramplesham as if I were some sort of a schoolboy just . . . Well, it puts me into the blue devils, and no mistake."

Much to her annoyance, Lizzie noticed that she had dropped a stitch. It was a moment or two before she trusted herself to speak. "Serena. Of course," she finally managed to say. "A most logical choice." She was surprised that her tone of voice was so neutral. Lady Serena Ramplesham, diamond of the first water, she of the blue-violet eyes and the breathless voice, had come out two years previously, in Elizabeth's Season, and had promptly eclipsed every other female upon the scene. The darling of her devoted papa the earl, she was, in Miss Webster's opinion, an accomplished flirt whose wilting airs in the presence of the opposite sex concealed a heart set only upon such worldly vanities as fortune, rank, title, and fashion, attributes which Lady Serena considered worthy tributes to her beauty. Perhaps because she was a cleric's daughter, Elizabeth's values were less material, but she could still not help but wonder at the values of a female who had set her cap first at a duke, then a marquis, then an earl, and failing to snare any of these matrimonial prizes, now seemed ready to settle upon a mere viscount whose personality and temperament were in every way opposite to her own. It also explained why George had been spending so much time in London this Season.

These and a number of other objections, far more personal, rose to Elizabeth's mind. But to her credit, she said nothing, when a mere whisper of criticism would have done, merely inquiring in a dispassionate tone of voice if George had indicated his interest to Lady Serena.

"Well, I think she knows from which corner the wind blows," George replied carefully. "Not that I've made a definite offer yet, you see, but I am planning on going to Bath before the harvest, because that's where Lord Ramplesham's in-laws are staying, see, and Lady Serena rather let drop that since she was so close, and her father would be there this fortnight next, that it might signify if I were to pay a call. She has not exactly been discouragin', you know," he added with a certain modest pride at having snared such a beauty. "Say, Lizzie, don't you think she's a bang-up sort of gal? I mean, a man could get lost in those eyes of hers, you know, and she's always turned out as fine as a fivepence, in the high crack of fashion."

What Lady Serena would think of becoming the bride of a man who would prefer to put on a reaper's smock and work in the fields with his men to making a leg at a fashionable *ton* party in London was something Elizabeth did not care to contemplate. She did not doubt, however, that George, who did not much care for the pleasures of fashionable society, would very soon find himself dancing attendance upon his intended at every smart drawing room in the metropolis, all the while wishing desperately that he were at home in Devon, sitting down to a plain dinner and a quiet evening by the fire.

"Thing of it is, you know, she's one who needs a man to carry her about." George was about to wax enthusiastic about his intended at great length, when their *tête-à-tête* was interrupted.

"Oh, I do say, I knew I would find you here, old boy," drawled Trevor Worthington to his cousin as he stepped through the doorway, resplendent in a bath coat of superfine, a pair of skintight nankeen breeches, and a pair of gleaming Hessians he considered suitable for country wear. " 'Servant, Lizzie! Trust you don't mind my dropping by like this, unannounced, but I heard the rector on the rumble, and decided I would just let myself in."

Oblivious of the flat stares he received from his cousin George and his childhood companion Miss Webster, Mr. Trevor Worthington paused to survey his neckcloth in the mirror above the table, satisfied that the height and expanse of its elaborate arrangement would in no way enable him to turn his head to the right or the left. As he picked imaginary specks of lint from the lapel of his jacket, George rolled his eyes expressively at Elizabeth, who, to suppress the unseemly laughter that rose to her lips, gathered her needlework rather close to her face for a moment.

It would never have occurred to Trevor Worthington to enter the rectory via the terrace doors, for to do so would have been to spot his boots with grass or mud. In feature, he bore much resemblance to his fraternal cousin George, but his countenance was of a finer sculpture, and his figure far more willowy than muscular, with the unhappy result that his tailor was forced to add a great deal of padding to his coat and his breeches. As he touched his pomaded curls, the strong odor of his cologne wafted across the room, and he regarded himself with a deep satisfaction. The perfection of his attire was something that occupied a great deal of Trevor's time, to the point of reglegating his other great interest, the pursuit of the female sex, to the background.

Having satisfied himself that he was in every way exquisite, Trevor turned from the mirror and walked with light, catlike steps toward Elizabeth, bowing over her hand in such a way that made George, not for the first time in his life, yearn to disarrange Trevor severely. His dislike was mirrored, although more subtly, in Elizabeth's eyes. Since earliest childhood, Trevor had not been the most popular member of their small circle. In fact, as George's late brother, Frederick, had been fond of saying, it was Trevor's lot in life to be the greatest snake in existence.

However much he might dislike Trevor, George had always been just a little in awe of his London-bred cousin's great air of fashion and sophistication—aptitudes to which he knew he could never aspire, and which, of late, in light of his courtship of Lady Serena, had taken on a dimension of desirability—so he watched with some interest as Trevor released Elizabeth's hand (which she surreptitiously wiped on her gown) and seated himself, without invitation, in the chair George had lately vacated.

"I think I will have a drop of Madeira if you

have it, and I see that you do, over there on the sideboard," he said.

Without missing a stitch, Elizabeth smiled thinly. "Then you will of course help yourself, Trevor," she said, and with a sigh he shifted himself out of the chair and edged toward the decanters.

George, seizing his chance, dropped his frame back into the chair Trevor had vacated and glared at his cousin.

"Well, my dears, the long and the short of it is, I've just come from Bath, and the *on-dit* is that a certain relation of mine is about to make an offer for a certain young and fashionable beauty."

"Who told you that?" George demanded.

Trevor poured his Madeira and sipped. "So nice, you know, that a parson should keep such a good cellar. I see that neither of you has a glass. May I?"

Both shook their heads, and Trevor replenished his own. "I also hear that a certain other lady may have her nose put sadly out of joint by this news," he added, looking directly at Elizabeth, who, to her great credit, returned his look with such a bland stare of idle curiosity that he merely waved a well-manicured hand in the air and continued. "That, however, has nothing to do with my business with you, George," he said quickly, just as George was about to demand the name of this other lady. "The thing of it is, old boy, I find myself in a bit of a jam, and this being one of those glorious autumn days when one simply *has* to put in a few hours in the country, if only to give one's leaders a head, I thought I would drive down and have a look-in on you."

"What do you want, Trevor?" Elizabeth asked flatly. It had always annoyed her dreadfully that Trevor seemed to be able to impose upon his cousin's good nature in the most remarkable ways. It was all she could do to restrain herself from delivering a stinging set-down as Trevor blithely continued onward, unheeding.

"When I found myself upon the horns of my dilemma, I rode like the wind from Bath to Ventor, because I knew you would help. And a damned inconvenient ride it was, too, if you must know the truth. Your servants have never liked me, George, and I have never been able to determine why. Could it be that they still cherish a grudge about that under-house-parlormaid after all these years?"

"How much do you need this time, Trev?" George asked patiently.

Trevor's elegant shoulders rose slightly in his jacket and he raised an eyebrow. "Money? Oh, no, nothing like that. I was quite lucky at Newmarket, you know. Oh, no, nothing at all like that. If Lizzie doesn't mind my plain speaking—and I am certain, in your ministrations to the poor and amoral, my dear, you have heard it all ... Well! The thing of it is, old boy, after much nattering about and putting on die-away airs, a certain bit of feminine grace has finally decided to elude her great beast of a husband and be my guest at my little *pied-à-terre* outside Bath."

"I suppose you are to be congratulated," Elizabeth remarked dryly. 'Although I must say I doubt the lady's taste."

Trevor picked up his quizzing glass and attempted to focus a single hideously magnified eye in Elizabeth's direction, but found himself unequal to outcountenancing the flat basilisk gaze of a rector's daughter offended. "What you think or do not think is of no consequence whatsoever, Lizzie," Trevor snapped, his elegant composure severely ruffled. It had always been thus between them since childhood.

"Anyway," he sighed, redirecting his attention toward George, long since inured to their squabbles, "the thing of it is, I find myself with a previous engagement. A summons from m'mother, you see, demanding my attendance at a reception she's throwing at Worthington House. Such a dead bore, you know, something to do with m'father being *such* a crony of the Prince Regent, and *tout le monde* being so *dégagé* with Prinny for his Turkish treatment of Princess Charlotte after she cried off from her engagement to Orange. Well, m'mother feels someone has to put on a show of support for father and daughter, even though *everyone* knows they're at daggers-drawn with each other." Wearily Trevor waved a pale hand in the air to indicate his complete disinterest in the affairs of the royal family.

Elizabeth, whose heart was tender toward practically everyone in the world except Trevor, sighed. "*Poor* Princess Charlotte! One does feel for her, you know, raised up as little better than a pawn between her parents, and now a pawn between her father and the Opposition. One hears that she is virtually a *prisoner* at Cranbourne Lodge, all of her own people removed from her and replaced with her father's spies, reporting upon her every action to him, odious creature that he is!"

George expressed the opinion of the nation: "It's all a great lot of damned foolishness to me." A sudden and terrible thought occurred to him, and he looked at Trevor narrowly, his good-natured face closed. "Now, dammit, Trevor, if you think for one moment that I'm going to travel all the way to London and truck myself out in knee breeches and all my orders just to stand around Aunt Augusta's house and attend one of those damned dull political parties just so you can—"

Trevor smiled beatifically. "I knew you would see it my way! George, you always were the very best of fellows! Why, it's practically your duty as head of household and all of that. It's tomorrow night at eight, and be there on time. You know how much Mama hates tardiness, particularly when the Prince is coming!"

Elizabeth rolled her eyes.

"Shall a man profit by the gleanings of others and expect a place in heaven?" the rector's voice demanded, ringing through the house.

2

Worthington House, a stolid, imposing Palladian mansion on Grosvenor Square, was illuminated from top to bottom that evening, and it might have seemed to a less prosaic person than Lord Ventor, strolling from his rooms at the Albany, that at least some of the light emanated from the very august assembly who clustered in the enormous state salons awaiting the appearance of the guests of honor.

Markedly uncomfortable in his dark evening rig of deep corbeau, even though it had come from his favorite tailor, and very much disliking the custom of wearing knee breeches and stockings for formal evenings, he made his way through the assembly to the place at the top of the stairs where his aunt and uncle stood receiving guests, a decidedly unpleasant expression marring his usually sunny countenance.

"Ah, George." His uncle greeted him without surprise, wringing his hand in a hearty grasp. "Trevor set you up, no doubt," he said. guessing the situation immediately.

George regarded his uncle without affection. A large florid man with the same dissipated look about him as his crony the Prince Regent, he had never quite adjusted to the idea that any nephew of his might prefer the life of a country gentleman to the delights of town. However, rumor had reached his ears, and he had high hopes that George might at last be settling into the family routine. "Are you to be congratulated, hey?" he asked with a broad wink. "Lady Serena's quite the taking little thing, y'know, and ten thousand a year's not to be taken lightly!"

Before George could make a reply, he was seized upon by his aunt, a hawk-nosed woman of greater height than her husband, made taller still by the inclusion of the triple plumes of Wales thrust into her purple turban. "I swear," she announced briskly, "I shall wring Trevor's neck! How *could* he do this to me? It is above all things outrageous that he should send you to us, George, instead of appearing here himself!" Since Augusta was rumored to have enjoyed more than a casual friendship with the future King of England herself, it was perhaps fortunate that Trevor bode fair to resemble her rather than his father. "And anyway, what's this

I hear about your offering for that Ramplesham chit? Her mother was a mushroom, one of the Yorkshire heiresses, y'know, when all the world knows that Lizzie Webster's been only waiting for you to say the word anytime these past two years!"

George forced a smile. "Utter nonsense, Aunt Augusta, I assure you! Lizzie's not the marryin' kind. Lady Serena's very much the thing, I assure you!"

"Perhaps a bit too much the thing!" Lady Worthington returned baldly. "She would do better with a husband like Trevor—be few illusions there on either side, and she'd be twice as fashionable! Think upon it!" With these words, she dismissed her nephew and turned toward the next guest, leaving him to wander off in search of a familiar face.

Unfortunately, there were none present, and it came as a great relief to him when at last there was a hush over the squeeze, and royalty made its appearance. At least now he could procure a glass of wine, he thought, lingering at the edge of the crowd as his aunt led her guests through the rooms.

Time and self-indulgence had ruined the face and figure of a man once said to have been the handsomest gentleman in Europe, and his stays squeaked alarmingly as he made his courtly bows to the ladies presented to him, but, observing him closely for the first time in his life, rather than at the distance of parade mount, George was not oblivious of the fact that the man was possessed of a great deal of charm when he chose to use it. Tonight he definitely chose to use it, and when he was introduced to Lord Ventor, he was all affability and readiness to please, standing upon little ceremony and inquiring closely after George's experiences in Spain and the fate of Ventor Hall, recalling George's father with a great deal of genuine affection, and presenting his son with one or two incidents that served to show his father in a far better light than George himself recalled his unfond parent.

But it was the Princess Charlotte, when his aunt presented him to her, who caught his attention and his sympathy. She was a tall female, with speaking eyes and an excellent complexion. Tonight, however, as George made his bow over her outstretched hand, he noticed that all those huge Hanoverian blue eyes seemed to speak about was a certain misery and boredom such as he had seen in the eyes of soldiers too long confined to barracks.

Unbecomingly attired in a gown of mauve satin and black lace, she was at all times flanked by her twin guardians, two old tabbies if ever George knew the breed, introduced to him as Ladies Ilchester and Rosslyn, who permitted her no more than a minute or two of conversa-

tion, closely monitored, with any single gentleman she might have honored with her notice.

Something in George's heart was touched by
the princess's plight. At eighteen, she should
have been going to parties and balls, flirting
gaily and dancing all night like other girls of
her generation, instead of being put out on a
chain like a bear and dragged through stuffy
assemblies of the elderly and powerful such as
this one of his aunt's. To be honest, her situation reminded him of his own, for there were
times when he too felt a prisoner of rank and
duty for which he had little taste, and, making idle conversation, he remarked in response
to some comment of hers, "I believe, ma'am,
that we have an acquaintance in common in Miss
Mercer Elphinstone. She was at school with
my sister, Lady Denholm, you see."

"Ah, Peg!" The princess's face lit up warmly,
and he realized he had touched upon a subject
dear to her heart. "Is she not the most capital
horsewoman, Lord Ventor? Have you ever seen
her drive four-in-hand?"

George returned her smile. "Indeed, there
was a time when she and m'sister put m'father
in a rage by taking out his high-perch phaeton
and bowling down the drive four-in-hand! They
were in high gig, let me assure you , ma'am!"

The princess gave a hearty peal of rich laughter. "If only you could see me with *my* team,"
she began, and then, perhaps recalling that

driving out behind her yellow-wheeled phaeton was one of the pleasures forbidden to her
of late, frowned slightly. But laughter was
enough to summon the twin guardians to her
side, and with the repressive glares of a pair of
Ming lions, they bore their charge away to
dance attention upon an elderly dowager with
an ear trumpet. Charlotte gave only the brief-
est of regretful glances over her shoulder, and
George was not entirely certain that, given her
own choice, she would have remained to en-
gage him in a lively discussion of horses, a
subject upon which she was reputed to be an
expert.

His duty done, George sighed with relief,
turning his finger inside his high cravat. One
more glass of champagne and he could take his
leave of his aunt, slipping out a side door to
have a look in at his old barracks and a comfortable visit with his old friends in the offi-
cers' mess, where, he had no doubt, his mission
upon the morrow, to stop at Bath and call
upon Lady Serena Ramplesham, would be
greeted with cheers and toasts.

3

One toast to the future happiness of the erstwhile Colonel Ventor had led to another, and another, and several more thereafter, with the consequence that George arose much later than was his custom and in no very good frame of mind, as the steward of his club could attest when he presented his lordship with a hearty English breakfast of kidneys, kippers, toast, and scrambled eggs in the morning only to be told, with no roundaboutation, to remove those blasted yellow things from his sight before he cast up his accounts.

It was therefore closer to noon than nine when George's phaeton and team were brought around, and George, his head still ringing from the previous evening's celebrations, threw himself up into the seat and wended his way through the city, hoping open air would clear his head before he reached Bath that evening.

It was only when he was approaching the Bristol Road that he noted a cotter pin was loosening itself from the forewheel of his carriage, and, bethinking his postponed breakfast, stopped at the White Hart, the great posting inn, in order to repair both himself and his phaeton.

Several cups of strong black coffee and a breakfast of fried tomatoes, cheese, and ham made him feel very much more the thing, and after paying his shot, he strolled out into the innyard to reclaim his phaeton, little dreaming that the events of the next quarter-hour were about to alter his life forever.

The great old stagecoach the Bristol Flier had arrived, and a number of persons from all degrees of life were milling about in the innyard, together with their bandboxes, portmateaux, and other belongings, including several crates of honking geese, all awaiting the coachman's call to board.

As he was paying off the smith, and wishing he had brought Silsby, his groom, there was a great shout of laughter from the assembled crowd around the lumbering mail coach, and George, paying attention for the first time, noticed that an altercation of some sort was in process between the sturdy old coachman and a young girl in a drab pelisse who looked, beneath her chip-straw bonnet, oddly familiar.

"You don't seem to understand, missy," John

Coachman was saying as he lifted a foaming tankard to his lips, clearly enjoying his role in this little drama. "You've a-purchased yerself a bill for an *inside* seat."

The girl, clutching a bandbox against herself and looking right into the coachman's eye, stamped her foot. "But it is my *wish* to sit on the outside!" she declared in ringing tones.

The coachman stroked his several chins, and there was snickering among the crowd. "You don't understand, missy," he repeated slowly, removing an ancient and much-folded sheet of paper from a capacious pocket of his greatcoat and running a thick finger over the print. "Hit states right here in the rules that bills of passage purchased between London and Bath for seats inside or out shall be honored as seats inside or out."

"Ought to be driven to Bedlam, she ought," interjected a stout farm wife carrying a crate of geese in her arms. "Anyone that can afford an inside seat and *wants* to sit out must be touched in the noggin."

The hostlers chuckled, elbowing each other and making rude comments. Two spots of color appeared in the girl's cheeks, and she drew herself up to her full height, which was oddly familiar to George. "I *command* you to allow me to sit on the outside!" she cried in clear, precise tones such as had never emitted from the mouth of a maid wearing a drab pelisse and a chip-straw bonnet. "I don't give a fig for the heat and dust! I want to sit on the outside!"

Suddenly George knew where he had heard that voice and seen that tall figure before—less than twenty-four hours ago in his aunt's state rooms at Worthington House. "Good God!" he said aloud, quite startled, and strode across the cobblestones to have a better look, quite sure that his blue devils had gotten to him at last.

"If you please, my good man," he said, elbowing aside a gaping rustic attending to this scene with a finger firmly in his nostril.

"I don't care what you want, missy! Rules is rules, and I've got the book to prove it so!" the coachman was saying, clearly losing patience.

"Listen to her talk, quality-like!" the stout farmwoman exclaimed. "I'll lay even money that she's running away from home! Someone ought to fetch the constables!"

The young girl flushed even deeper, and gave the farmwoman a haughty stare. "That is not at all true!" she exclaimed, clutching her bandbox even closer to her chest. "I am a respectable ladies' maid, on my way to fill a post at Bath!"

As she lifted the bandbox, George knew with an awful certainty that this was no blue devil's dream, but really happening, for he knew, as well as any other British subject, the gold crest stamped upon the side of the box.

Peering closely at the young female, he also recognized that the drab pelisse and the chip-straw bonnet were a thin disguise, for the girl was none other than Princess Charlotte herself, apparently running away again.

In general, George was not a quick thinker, but on the field of battle he had more than once been mentioned in dispatches for his talent of quickly rising to the occasion.

"So! Here I find you!" he announced in stentorian tones learned from years of listening to the rector's sermons, as he shouldered his way through the crowd and grasped the heiress to the throne of England, Scotland, Ireland, and Wales by the arm. "Running away, are you? Well, we'll see about that! You maybe certain that this time Papa will lock you up on bread and water for a week and prevent you from attending any balls for a month!" He looked about at the crowd. The princess, speechless with surprise, made no protest. "My sister," he explained as he dragged her away across the courtyard and all but threw her into his phaeton, climbing aboard and whipping up his leaders to a spanking pace before anyone could make the least outcry.

"Really, ma'am," he said a little breathlessly, "if you insist upon running away, at least make your disguise plausible enough to pass muster!

The first rule of disguise is never, ever make yourself conspicuous. If you were a spy, you'd have been shot by now!"

The princess, adjusting her skirts about her, regarded him with something akin to admiration. "Thank you," she said at last. "I shall remember that! Ah, it is Lord . . . Lord Ventor, is it not? Peggy Mercer Elphinstone's friend?"

"At your service, Ma'am," George replied, tipping his hat.

"Good!" Charlotte replied, entirely satisfied. "Then you may take me to Bath, if you please. I have been badly used, and I am going to the home of my old governess, Mrs. Campbell, until my father sees reason!"

"On the contrary, ma'am," George replied firmly, "you are going directly back to Cranbourne Lodge, Windsor, where I shall place you in the hands of your guardians with as little scandal as can be attached to my name or yours! *I* am going to Bath to propose to Lady Serena Ramplesham, and not even a runaway princess can stop me today!"

"Can't I just?" Charlotte asked, crossing her arms over her chest. "Lord Ventor, I *command* you, as a royal princess— *your* princess, sir!—to take me to Bath."

"Ma'am," George said, attempting to maintain a reasonable tone of voice against all odds, "your father is my sovereign, and should I convey you to Bath, I'm . . . well, I'm not quite sure what would happen to me, but I can promise you it would be dashed unpleasant. High treason or some such thing."

"It doesn't signify," the princess replied airily. "Since I shall become queen and immediately set you free!"

"Can you reattach my head to my body? I mean, ma'am, at the very least, you know, I could be transported to the antipodes for kidnapping an heiress!"

"Lady Serena Ramplesham must be a very dull stick indeed, to attach herself to a man with so little sense of the romantic as you," Charlotte retorted, tilting her chip-straw hat down over her eyes in a decisive fashion.

"Not a dull stick at all!" George protested. "She's an accredited beauty!"

Her royal highness made a very rude noise and leaned back against the seat, her chin thrust determinedly outward as she calculated Lord Ventor from beneath the brim of her hat. "I shall join my mother in Italy," she announced. "Surely *she* will have me, when she sees how ill-used I am become in my own country and by my own father."

George, reflecting that the last thing he had heard about the princess's estranged mother, Caroline of Brunswick, was that that lady was traveling about Italy in a white phaeton drawn by a matched team of white horses driven by a child dressed as a cherub in company with person named Bergami, was wise enough to hold his tongue upon that score. When it came to the question of the princess's parents, it was his opinion that one was as bad as the other. But their affairs troubled him not one-half as much as the product of their disastrous marriage, sitting up beside him, driving through the very public streets of London dressed in a drab pelisse and a chip-straw bonnet, looking more and more as if she were about to burst into tears the closer they came to Windsor. Not that he could blame her, but driving about the streets of London with a weeping woman in an open phaeton was certain to draw a great deal of unfavorable attention, perhaps even rec-ognition of the lady in question, who must certainly already be missed.

"If you will only not make a watering pot of yourself," he finally promised in desperation as they rounded Temple Bar, where he could easily see his severed head being displayed over the gates, "I shall provide you with a luncheon, and we shall try to work this damned tangle out. If only Lizzie were here, she would know precisely what to do!"

Her royal highness, accepting the clean hand-kerchief he offered her, blew her nose and dabbed her eyes. "I thought her name was Serena," she pointed out, a little heartened by the thought of a meal.

"That's someone else," George said absently.

"Lizzie is my friend. A great go! You would like her immensely—everyone does."

"Then if I were you, I should offer for her instead of this Lady Serena," her royal highness remarked, somewhat diverted from her own problems.

"If you will forgive me for saying so, ma'am, it's none of your business," George announced firmly as they pulled into the yard of White's Hotel, a most respectable, if not highly fashionable establishment. Here, at least, there would be no chance of either of them being recognized among the barristers and solicitors having their midday meal during recess at the Old Bailey.

He was able, without a great deal of curiosity being aroused, to procure a private parlor, and ordered himself a tankard of ale while he watched his princess devour a most hearty luncheon.

"I haven't eaten anything since last night," she said, having removed her chip-straw bonnet in order to attack a plate of cold roast beef and Stilton cheese. "I must say your aunt's lobster patties were a trifle *dry*," she added.

"My aunt likes to pare the cheese when she can," George admitted.

"Is it true that she and my father were once—"

"Tell me how you came to make your escape," George said abruptly, forestalling any further embarrassing questions.

The princess chuckled. "I stole the hat and pelisse from a lady-in-waiting's maid," she said baldly. "Well, I did leave her a perfectly nice blue velvet habit in place of it, but since I doubt she rides, I don't know what she'll make of it. Everyone thought I was somewhere else, you see. The grooms thought I was practicing my French, and my French master thought I was out riding, and Lady Ilchester thought I was with Lady Rosslyn, and Lady Rosslyn thought I was with Lady Ilchester, and no one, you know, looks at a lady's maid, so out I went through the service entrance and that was that. It was remarkably easy. I wonder that I never thought of it before." She was, George realized, quite pleased with herself, as would be any chit of eighteen who had managed to elude an overstrict governess for an afternoon.

"But you must stop and think about the consequences of your own actions, you know," George said slowly. "You're not just some runaway Bath miss, ma'am—you're . . . well, you're *you*. This will cause a great deal of scandal, you know."

She turned her enormous blue eyes upon him. "All the world must know, my lord," she said slowly, "how ill-used I am! All it would take would be for me to stand up and declare myself to that common room of lawyers as ill-used and escaping from the tyranny of my father, who despises me, to incite a mob to storm Carlton House this very afternoon! And it would serve him right, too, him and that fat cow, Lady Coyningham!"

George was forced to acknowledge the truth of what she said. Never had the Regent's popularity been so low as it was at the present time, his mistresses and his excesses flaunted in the face of a nation plunged into a depressive postwar economy, and never had his daughter been so popular. Since she had broken off her engagement to the Prince of Orange and run away to Connaught Place to her mother two years earlier, she had been more or less a prisoner of state.

All of these things George, and every other Englishman, knew, but being faced with the lady herself was an entirely different manner.

"I do wish you would stop such fustian nonsense," George had the wit to say, "for if you were to go into the common-room and proclaim yourself Princess of Wales, it's more likely they'd storm Bedlam than Carlton House."

Her royal highness bit her lip thoughtfully, considering this piece of information, before digging into a plate of fresh apple tarts, her appetite unimpaired. "*All* I really want, you see, is to go and stay with my old governess, Mrs. Alicia Campbell, in Bath. She at least understands me. If Prince Leopold were here, he would have no hesitation in conveying me thence, you know."

"Well, I don't know this Prince Leopold fella, but it seems to me if he cared about you, he'd take you right straight back to your father, and the less said about it, the better. Only recall, ma'am, what a merry time there was when you ran off to your mother's in Connaught Place!"

"My personal affairs are none of your concern," her royal highness said, every inch the princess, and George inclined his head slightly. "Besides," she added wistfully, "if Mrs. Campbell were about, she would not force me to be bear-led about Cranbourne, and to be so illused!" A large tear rolled down her cheek, and looking out the window at a pair of shopgirls walking arm-in-arm down the street, she added, "Oh, what I would give to be plain Miss No One of Nowhere!"

Perhaps it was the threat of more tears, perhaps it was because Lord Ventor was so inexperienced in the handling of young ladies, or perhaps it was a simple sympathy with his future sovereign and her desire to be a plain, ordinary person, a feeling he had cherished himself since the unhappy course of events had thrust his peerage so unexpectedly upon him. Perhaps it was merely some imp of perversity in what was otherwise an entirely goodnatured and prosaic soul. Whatever, he was astonished to hear his own voice. "I should be pleased to convey you to Mrs. Campbell in Bath, since I myself am heading in that direction to make my proposal to Lady Serena Ramplesham!"

"Oh, Lord Ventor!" exclaimed Charlotte, throwing her arms impulsively about his neck. "You are as great a hero as Byron or Scott ever wrote about! I promise you, sir, when it is in my power, I shall not forget this day!"

"Oh, I , er, well!" George said, blushing a deep red. "I rather hope so, for if my part in all of this is discovered, you may be certain that it will be *my* head on a pike at Temple Bar!"

Charlotte, tying the ribbons of her bonnet beneath her chin, smiled sunnily at him, all tears gone. "Well, then I shall command you to transport me to Bath, and you shall have to do so, and it will thus lay upon me. After all, sir, no one would behead you! This *is* the nineteenth century and modern times!"

4

The heiress apparent enjoyed a considerable reputation as a superb horsewoman, but George, who also was possessed of his admirers as a horseman, refused to allow her to take the reins until they had passed through the last suburbs of the metropolis and come into the open country, and even then, not without considerable pleading.

Princess Charlotte, however, soon aquitted herself with dispatch, so much so that George was grudgingly compelled to compliment her upon her skill and style, even as he offered, from time to time, some critical advice, to which she responded with such respectful docility that their relationship soon abandoned formality, and they found themselves upon the terms of an older brother who has unexpectedly released his young sister from the confines of a strict school for an unexpected holiday.

The countryside was touched with the first full bloom of autumn color, and the day bright and sunny, with a pleasant warmth that allowed George to relax against the seat and fall into a half-drowse that did something to cure the last vestiges of the blue devils still tormenting him from the excesses of the night before. Being possessed of a sanguine temperament and in perfect expectation that history would vindicate this single irrational act of a long and entirely rational life and that the good Mrs. Campbell of Laura Place would soon have possession of her charge, he was suddenly startled from his torpor by the sound of a coachman's horn blasting very near his ear, and opened his eyes to find her royal highness, with a perfectly serene expression upon her face, hauling his phaeton and four past the lumbering Bristol Mail so closely that he could make out the scratches in the coach's varnish as they passed. He saw, further, that a deep ditch lay on the other side of the phaeton and that the left wheels wobbled precariously upon the edge of this channel as Charlotte pulled ahead with a flick of the whip over the ear of the leader and pulled into the lane ahead of the Mail's horses with inches to spare, just as a farm cart came lumbering down the road toward them.

George, hanging on to his high-crowned beaver for dear life, uttered some properly military phrases more suitable to the barracks than the ears of the princess royal, who merely chortled as she rounded a corner and reduced her team to a more sedate pace. "By heaven," she announced, "now, that was a great go, my lord!"

"A great go it would have been if you had thrown us into a ditch, my girl!" George exclaimed, abandoning all formality in his anger.

He was rewarded with a rich Hanoverian chuckle. "But I did not, did I?" she asked, keeping her eye on the road, a portrait of feminine docility as she allowed him to retrieve the reins from her hands. "I can drive to an inch, you know. Papa made me drive in and out of a field gate until I could contrive to do so without scraping the sides of a pony cart."

"Be that as it may," George informed her sternly, "it would have been a fine thing, ma'am, if you were to throw us over and break your royal neck! *That* I could not be held accountable for!"

"No, of course not," the princess agreed meekly, but there was still a gleam of mischief in her eye.

"Still and all," George said when they had passed some distance in silence, "it *was* a great go, ma'am!"

"Thank you, sir," Charlotte replied with a

suitable modesty thoroughly overthrown by her impish grin.

They were able to journey into Bath without further incident, but George began to think that it would be a very good thing to deposit the spirited and hoydenish young lady into the care of a governess, for certainly *he* was not cut out for such adventures.

Twilight was just descending upon that lovely city, bathing it in a golden glow, when George brought his phaeton up before the tiny town house on Laura Place. He had a faint and unhappy feeling that his troubles were just beginning, however, when he noted that the knocker had been removed from the door, and no lights shone from any of the curtained windows.

"I shall be so anxious to see dear Campy," Charlotte said, and again George was startled by the naiveté of everyday things her sheltered upbringing had protected her from.

"It would appear, ma'am, that she may not be at home," he said doubtfully, leaping from the perch and striding up the walk, where he gave several sharp raps on the door and waited for an interminable length of time before an aged caretaker grudgingly cracked an opening and peered outside.

"I have come upon important business for Mrs. Alicia Campbell," George announced.

"She's gone," replied the shrouded figure in

senile tones, and made to shut the door again, but not before George could thrust his boot into the opening.

"Well, my good man, where has she gone? This is an important matter, involving a former charge of hers."

The grizzled old face peered myopically at him, clearly unimpressed. "Well, she ain't here," he said, "an' I'd thank yew to get yer foot outta my door!"

George, assailed by the very strong fumes of gin, was hard pressed to conceal the dismay on his open countenance as it began to sink in upon him that the lady whom he sought might not be returning.

"Well," he said, exasperated, "can you at least give me her direction?"

The grizzled retainer scratched his head doubtfully. "Seems to me, sir, I'd be hard pressed to recall proper where Mrs. C. went without a spot of gin to clear me memory, if you was to take my meaning," he added, peering over George's shoulder at the figure in the drab pelisse, who had jumped down from the phaeton and was walking the team in an expert fashion. The lascivious chuckle he emitted in no way mollified Lord Ventor, but seeing no other choice, George produced a guinea from his purse and found it snatched from his hand by gnarled and none-too-clean fingers. A single tooth in the ancient's mouth tested the weight of the coin before the caretaker replied, "Mrs. Campbell has gone on a walking tour of the Lake District and she won't be back for a fortnight."

"Two weeks—" George was exclaiming as the door was firmly shut in his face. He felt as if someone had ripped a rug out from beneath his feet, and frowning, he thrust his hands into his pockets and turned away from the door, suddenly aware of the interested stares he was receiving from Mrs. Campbell's neighbors on Laura Place.

Slowly he turned and walked down the stairs, his face a study in bemusement as he approached the princess. "Whatever do you think you're doing?" he demanded.

"Walking the team, of course," she replied. "One should never leave a heated horse standing, especially on a night like this. I am surprised that you do not travel with your groom, my lord."

"Best you should be glad," George replied gloomily, helping her back up into her seat and resuming his own. "If Potter were to see the pickle I am in now, you may be assured that he would leave my employ in disgust. Mrs. Campbell is on a walking tour of the Lake District, and will not be back for another fortnight!"

If he expected this news to daunt his royal companion, he was sadly mistaken. Retying the strings of her bonnet, she was unfazed. "Then perhaps we ought to venture in that direction next," she suggested.

"Out of the question!" George replied. "First, it is two days' journey from here, and second, we should never find her! A walking tour of the Lake District is likely to take one anywhere!"

Charlotte was forced to acknowledge the truth of this, adding that Mrs. Campbell was an inveterate walker. "However, it is of no consequence!" she added. "We shall simply put up at a hotel. I believe it is quite unexceptionable— why, the czar himself stayed at a hotel when he came to London and put Papa in such a passion—or rather his sister did, you know."

George's sense of propriety, already overheated by the events of the day, was now completely outraged. "Ma'am! That would never do." he informed her, much shocked. "Only consider that by now your parent must have everyone in the country alerted to your disappearance—no young lady could hope to put up at a respectable hotel without so much as a maid to keep her chaperoned, much less with a single gentleman as her only escort! You would be discovered and my head would be placed on a pike at Traitors' Gate!"

"Well, we could use assumed names, of course. I believe I read about some such thing in a romance once. Or perhaps it was a play. Whatever it was, it was jolly good, you know."

"Well, it won't do," George replied firmly. "Only consider the scandal of it all! Heiress apparent and all of that! Not to mention what Lady Serena would say to me!" A sudden thought occurred to him, and his face cleared instantly. "Of course, I should have thought of it at once! Best thing to do! Put you in the charge of Lady Ramplesham! Unexceptionable sort of female ... well, a bit of a high stickler, actually, but all things considered, what other choice do we have? Yes, I think the best course is to deliver you to the Rampleshams!"

"But I am not at all certain I want to be delivered to the Rampleshams!" Princess Charlotte protested. "Consider, sir, that I have run away from one form of captivity—and not in order to be placed in another!"

"Oh, quite respectable people, the Rampleshams! Be thrilled to have a princess of the blood under their roof," George said, but there was a tiny feeling of doubt in his mind when he considered the very formidable propriety of his future mother-in-law.

He could not, at that moment, however, think of any other way out of his difficulties, and in the blind faith of his love for the beautiful Lady Serena, was disinclined to see that she might have another reaction than his own, once he had explained it all to her.

Therefore, he wheeled his wearying horses around to the Ramplesham house on Sydney

Gardens, and was gratified to find that here, at least, there was a light in the window and the lion's-head knocker of highly polished brass was hung on the front door.

As he assisted the princess down, George remarked, "Well, you don't look very much like royalty, but I daresay we shall have to explain it all as it happened anyway, and Lady Serena will not mind *too* much."

"If she does not mind you, my lord, in all your dirt," Charlotte replied equably, smoothing out her gloves, "I am sure she will not mind me in mine. As you say, Lady Serena must be a paragon of every virtue."

Offering the princess his arm, George strode manfully up to the house and knocked smartly upon the lion's-head knocker, but his confidence was somewhat diminished when the door was opened by Phipps, the Rampleshams' funereal and august butler, whose brows had to rise only a fraction of an inch in order to betray his dismay at the sight of the gentleman whom the entire household expected to affiance himself to Lady Serena, not only appearing in a decidedly travel-worn condition, but with what Phipps could only describe as a Young Person in his company.

"Good evening, Phipps," George said briskly. "I trust that Lady Serena is in?"

The famous eyebrows moved up another quarter of an inch. It was a look that was rumored to have blasted chambermaids into floods of tears, but George nobly stood his ground.

"If I may be permitted to say so, my lord," Phipps confided as he stepped aside to allow George and her royal highness to enter the hall, "you were expected a great deal earlier in the day, and *alone*. Lady Serena may not be in the very best of moods, you understand."

George understood all too well, and a slight look of dismay filtered across his face. "Well, I think when she understands the circumstances that have delayed me, there will be no cause for anxiety. But I must speak with her privately, you understand, Phipps. The matter is of the utmost delicacy."

Once again a golden guinea changed hands, and Phipps was more inclined to nod understandingly. "Indeed, sir, and shall I place the Young Person in the library while you and Lady Serena interview in the Gold Salon?"

George shook his head. "No, no, she must see us both! Otherwise she might not believe . . . that is, you will be good enough to go find Lady Serena and tell her that I must see her at once?"

The eyebrows slid up another quarter of an inch, particularly when Charlotte giggled at being described as a Young Person, but after having deposited George and her royal highness in the Gold Salon, a very modern room done up in touches of yellow and crimson, Phipps took himself off to find Lady Serena.

"And Lord Ventor always seemed like such a calm sort of gentleman," a footman heard him murmuring abstractedly as he moved on his funereal tread down a corridor.

Petted and cosseted from birth by her indulgent parents, and made much of for her famous beauty by almost everyone since she was in leading strings, Lady Serena Ramplesham made no attempt to conceal her annoyance when Phipps announced that Lord Ventor awaited her in the Gold Salon. She had just finished dressing for dinner and a concert following in Sydney Gardens, and having waited all day for George to appear, was inclined to pay him back in his own coin, for she was not used to being kept waiting by anyone, most particularly a man who, by all indications, intended to make her an offer. Although she found his cousin Trevor Worthington far more attractive, Lady Serena, two Seasons out, was willing to overlook such small matters as love and attraction in favor of the rank and status that would attach to herself as Lady Ventor. She did not need the hints dropped into her ear by her mama that, the duke and the earl having failed to come up to scratch, it behooved her to entertain the viscount without any of her usual flirtations and games. Nor did she need to be reminded that there was only a mere baronet waiting in the wings. Allowing her maid to fasten a choker of seed pearls about her lovely neck, she paused only long enough to imbibe deeply of her own beauty in the pier glass, and content that she was, as usual, a Vision in a dress of celestial blue trimmed with silver net that set off her milky white skin and blue-black hair to perfection, she curtly dismissed her abigail, fortunately missing the sulky look that damsel shot her back, and after pinching her cheeks to assure a pleasing blush, descended the stairs with every expectation of receiving a proposal of marriage from an adoring Lord Ventor, and mentally planning how she meant to punish him only a little for making her wait all day long for his arrival.

Phipps, who was the soul of tact, had neglected to mention that milord had arrived in all his dirt, accompanied by a Young Person in a chip-straw bonnet and a drab pelisse, so when Lady Serena glided on silver slippers into the Gold Salon, her entrance was somewhat spoiled by the sight of this pair hovering by the cold fireplace.

As George turned from the princess, Lady Serena stiffened, her lovely little nose quivering with indignation as she stared down its length at Charlotte, who returned her look with a disconcerting frankness not to be expected from strange females in unfashionable attire.

"Serena ... thank God!" George uttered,

hardly noticing that the gloved hand he grasped in his own was stiff and unyielding. "I knew I could depend upon you!"

"Indeed," Lady Serena said coolly, surveying her suitor, from the tips of his muddy Hessians to the top of his disheveled curls, with a faintly curling lip. "The very least you could have done was change into evening clothes," she added coldly, withdrawing her hand from his, displeased at the smudge of dust on her three-button gloves.

George, flustered, took a step back, completely at a loss. Hitherto Lady Serena had been upon her very best behavior in their courtship, and the sight of her pretty face etched in ice was something he could have hardly been expected to comprehend as a warning sign.

"Your royal highness, may I present Lady Serena Ramplesham?" George continued, minding his manners.

Charlotte, having taken one look at the Beauty and sensed the direction in which the wind was blowing, graciously inclined her chip-straw bonnet. "Howyewdo?" she murmured without offering her hand, her blue eyes appraising Lady Serena with royal hauteur, as if this were one of her grandmother's drawing rooms.

Lady Serena, not fond of other women at the best of times, ignored the princess and turned to George, her mouth definitely set in lines of disapproval. "May I ask," she inquired in tones of glacial disdain, "if this is somehow your idea of a joke, Lord Ventor?"

George flushed to the roots of his hair. "Well, I'll admit that her royal highness doesn't precisely *look* like her royal highness, but it is she ... aren't you, ma'am?"

Charlotte, having taken an instant dislike to Lady Serena, merely inclined her head slightly, deeply offended at this lèse-majesté. "I am Charlotte Augusta, Princess of Wales," she announced, every inch the princess in spite of her attire.

Lady Serena flounced—there was no other word for it—toward George. "And I suppose you are Prinny himself!" she flared. "How dare you? How *dare* you?"

George put up his hands pleadingly. "Well, it's not that I dared, precisely ... well, I suppose I did, and I know it must look dashed odd, Serena, but she is, you know, the ... ah, princess!"

Lady Serena Ramplesham turned to ice from head to toe, quivering with indignation. "How could you serve me such a trick, sir? Are you run mad? Why, this ... this baggage could no more be the princess than ... than I could!"

Charlotte, completely unused to being addressed as a baggage and accused of being an impostor, drew herself up to her full height, which was considerably more than Lady Serena's. "Just as you wish, miss!" she drawled in haughty tones of utter contempt. "But I shall warn you, I am not used to being snubbed by a mere earl's daughter. You will be good enough to listen to what Lord Ventor has to say, if you please!"

"I think I would, if I were you, Serena," George gulped.

But Lady Serena Ramplesham, who had been brought up more as a princess than the princess herself, stamped a tiny foot. "How dare you? How *dare* you?" she cried.

It was the first time George had ever seen this side of his intended and he was not entirely certain that he liked it at all. Indeed, it possessed the power to terrify him. Had he known better, he would have realized that Lady Serena was upon the verge of throwing one of her famous temper tantrums.

"How dare you? How dare you?" she kept repeating, her eyes flashing. "First, you show up here hours and hours and hours late, and keep me waiting, and then you introduce *me* to this . . . this female as if she were the Princess of Wales! I will not have it! I will not! It is not at all the way in which I am to be treated!"

"Now, Serena," George said helplessly, "if you will but simply listen—"

"I am fairly certain, Lord Ventor, that Lady Serena is unwilling to listen to anything you are likely to say!" the princess exclaimed quickly. "In fact, I think we are both wasting

57

our time and jeopardizing our cause by attending to this chit one more minute!"

"Indeed you are!" Lady Serena's voice shook. "Out! Out! Out! I won't have it! I won't, I won't, I won't!" She strode across the room and reached for the bell-pull, but Phipps had obviously been lingering right outside the door, for he appeared with indecent haste.

"Yes, my lady?" he asked, his eyebrows practically in his hairline.

"Show Lord Ventor and . . . and his . . . his *doxy* to the door at once!" Lady Serena commanded.

"Serena, if you would only allow me to explain—"George pleaded, but Phipps had already given the signal to two of Lord Ramplesham's most burly footmen, and he found himself being hustled down the hallway and out the door before he could make any further protest.

"Does this mean that you don't wish to marry me?" he cried as the footmen ejected him out the door, Princess Charlotte, shaking off Phipps's hand, following.

His reply was the firm slam of that portal against him forever.

"Now see what you've done!" George said miserably to the princess as she helped to pick him up from the extremely undignified position he had landed in on the steps.

"Indeed, I am excessively sorry," Charlotte

said complacently, brushing him off with the fingers of her glove, "but somehow I do not think she would have done for you anyway."

"But I intended to ask her to be my wife!" George exclaimed unhappily, ignoring the stares of curious passersby on their way to the fireworks concert in the gardens across the street.

"Well, she may be pretty, but she is greatly spoiled and a ninnyhammer besides," Princess Charlotte replied with a great deal of surprising wisdom. "I daresay she would have made you entirely miserable with her fits and starts over the merest trifles! *I* should rather be thrown into the Tower than have such a poor spirit involved in my adventure!"

"Your adventure!" George exclaimed, getting painfully to his feet and examining the ruined crown of his beaver hat. "Your adventure? Good God, what a tangle you have landed me in, you wretched schoolgirl. Ma'am," he added, placing his hat on his head and glaring at her angrily.

"Well, it is considerably more of an adventure than anything else that has happened to me recently," Charlotte confided, completely unruffled, and with a sparkle in her fine blue eyes. "But if you consider that absolutely *nothing* ever happens to me, then I suppose that it must look rather dull to you."

"Dull? Good God!" George sighed, rubbing his body where it ached the most from his hasty ejection from the Ramplesham house. "I would rather be back in Spain fighting Boney than spend another hour with you!"

Charlotte looked at him thoughtfully, and then did a most unexpected thing. Slowly her blue eyes grew enormous, and several large tears spilled down her rosy cheeks. She neither sobbed nor heaved, simply allowed the tears to dribble down her face, with such a woebegone look on her face that George, whose heart was easily touched, immediately put a strengthening arm about her shoulders and dug in his pocket for his handkerchief, which he presented to her with a flourish. "Blow," he commanded, and she did so. "There, there, no need to fuss. It will all turn right, I promise you. I suppose I *might* have been mistaken in Lady Serena's character."

"She has none," the princess managed to say, looking at him over his handkerchief.

"Well, I wouldn't say that—such a trim little figure, such a pretty face," George said regretfully, which caused a renewal of Charlotte's tears, so much so that they were attracting the interest of passersby.

"Buck up, ma'am," George said, leading her across the street and into the gardens. "I daresay some victuals would not come amiss right now? There's a tiny café in the gardens where you might have an ice and a piece of pastry until dinnertime." George patted her in an affectionate sort of way. "Daresay we might even see some of the rockets, if you like."

"Then you are not angry with me?" the princess demanded.

George shrugged. "Not too very much, if you're not going to make a watering pot of yourself."

"Papa always says that is my very best trick," Charlotte replied serenely. "Not everyone can produce tears upon command, you know."

"What? You unprincipled little minx!" George exclaimed, gripping the princess unceremoniously by the arm and dragging her toward the waiting phaeton. "That rips it, by God it does, ma'am! If I must drive all night, I'll restore you instantly to your father at Brighton, by God I will! You may be who you are, but you've managed to ruin my life all right and tight!"

Unceremoniously he hoisted her up into the seat and took his own, still muttering some very dark things indeed. "To Brighton, then, and I hope that your father beats you with a riding crop!" he said darkly, although in reality he would have been horrified by such a development.

"And," her royal highness replied, completely unfazed, "when I am Queen of England, sir, I shall have you beheaded!" That she meant this no more than he wished corporal punishment upon her mattered not a trifle to either of them, for they were arguing like a sulky brother and sister. "Anyway, my lord," Charlotte added spiritedly, "Lady Serena Ramplesham never would have suited you at all, for when I am queen, I mean to cut her dead!"

"I am certain that she will be very much surprised!" George retorted furiously, hard pressed to suppress a chuckle at the expression that would no doubt be upon Lady Serena's lovely face when she attended her first royal drawing room and discovered that she had indeed insulted a royal personage. Soon, however, the thought of Darkest Scandal overtook him, and he lapsed into a gloomy silence, leaving Charlotte to imagine out loud all the most dreadful social consequences she would inflict upon the hapless Beauty when it was in her power to do so.

5

Although the princess was momentarily cast down by her companion's burst of temper, it was not long before they were on the high road, traveling along beneath the bright silver light of a full moon, when she could no longer keep silent. Unused to having her will thwarted by a mere peer, she crossed her arms over her drab pelisse and threw Lord Ventor a smoldering glance.

Lord Ventor, contemplating the thought that twenty-four hours ago his life had been as well ordered as any man could wish, and contrasting it with the events of this day, specifically his treatment at the hands of Lady Serena Ramplesham, was far too occupied with his own misery to notice the princess's displeasure until she spoke up in her most imperious tones.

"I do not *want* to go to Brighton! I will *not* go to Brighton! I command you to turn back and deposit me in a respectable hotel in Bath! At once!" she exclaimed, almost but not quite stamping one booted foot against the floorboards.

"Oh, be quiet, do! Can't you see that you've already landed us both in the soup!" George replied tartly, adding as an afterthought, "Ma'am!"

"I shall throw myself out of this carriage and onto the mercy of my people!" Charlotte declared melodramatically. "But I will not go to Brighton!"

"As a matter of fact, *I* don't want to go to Brighton either!" George retorted. "Doubtless I shall arrive there to find my head upon a pike, or worse! Don't know your father, but I'll imagine that he'll be ready to cast up my accounts—and yours too!"

"Precisely so!" Charlotte exclaimed. "That is why I intend to hurl myself out of this phaeton and upon the mercy of a passing stranger!"

"Much good that will do you," George replied prosaically. "Like as not, you'll break a leg or an arm and have to sit by the side of the road all night waiting for a carter or a farmer's gig to drive past. And then, like as not, if you were to proclaim yourself Princess of Wales, you'd be clapped into Bedlam or handed over to the magistrate!"

Charlotte, whose main move to hurl herself

from the phaeton had been to grasp the brass rail by her side, bit her lower lip, sulkily considering the truth of what George was representing to her.

"Then I command you to turn around at once and deposit me in a respectable hotel in Bath! I will wait there until Miss Campbell returns from her holiday!"

George shook his head. "Would that I could dispose of you so easily! Believe me, at this juncture nothing would give me more pleasure than to be thoroughly rid of you! But only consider, no respectable hotel would admit an unescorted female without so much as a maid to lend her countenance, let alone a chit of a girl in a drab pelisse and that quiz of a bonnet!"

"When they know that I am the Princess of Wales, they will!"

"And how are they to know that? And with what do you intend to pay for this prolonged stay? Do you have any money about you?"

From her momentary silence Lord Ventor assumed that her royal highness was without funds, and her next statement proved him correct.

"I never carry money. I never need to, you know. Royals do not, as a rule."

"There, you see! You're no more equipped to take care of yourself than a babe unborn!" George pointed out triumphantly. "Would you not prefer to be between clean sheets at Brighton than on the run?"

"Not if Lady Coyningham is there!" the princess retorted, and George, thinking of the Regent's latest mistress, said nothing. That, he decided, was not his problem.

"Well-brought-up young ladies do not discuss females such as Lady Coyningham," he said repressively, however, and received a droll chuckle in reply for his pains.

"It should be clear to all the world that I am *not* a well-brought-up young lady! I am the future Queen of England!"

"Just as you say, ma'am," George retorted oppressively. "And here we have the future Queen of England jaunting about the countryside with a half-blown viscount! The world turned upside down, indeed!"

"If you please, Lord Ventor, may I have the reins now? You're sawing away in a most unhappy manner every time you are out of temper!"

"I am not out of temper!" George exclaimed, turning to deliver her royal highness a singularly speaking look. "Well, if I am, it's to be laid at your door! How I ever allowed myself to be talked into anything so caper-witted, I do not know!"

"Prince Leopold would not consider it caper-witted! *He* is a man of spirit!" the princess retorted.

"Then I wish this Prince Leopold person were here instead of me, for I have never in my life embroiled myself in any project so ill-conceived as this!"

"No, I doubt that you have! Anyone who would propose to such an out-and-out rum-faced prig as Lady Serena Ramplesham would never have the *bottom* required of a true hero!"

"Oh, be quiet, do!" George exclaimed, and in doing so, turned to look at the princess in a darkling manner, completely missing the road sign, half-concealed behind overgrown shrubbery, which indicated that a turn in the high road to the left led to Brighton, while a right-hand fork led to Bristol. Unconsciously George reined his leader toward the right fork. If the princess noticed this mistake, she gave no sign, but a small and rather mischievous smile played about the corners of her lips nonetheless, and she cast her eyes from George to her hands, folded neatly in her lap.

"Just as you say, sir," she murmured.

Such was the essential tenderness of George's nature that he immediately felt regretful of his temper. "Well, there," he said awkwardly, "don't turn into a watering pot, I beg of you! Once in a day is enough! Didn't mean to speak so hard to you, ma'am, but only consider!"

"I am considering," Charlotte said softly, but what Lord Ventor mistook for shaking sobs were actually convulsions of laughter, which

67

Charlotte took due care to disguise behind her hands.

"There, now, it's not all that bad! I daresay your father will be so glad to see you again that he won't kick up the devil's own dust, you know! M'father used to come the ugly over one or two of my scrapes, but then he'd calm right down, you know, and all would be right in a trice! You'll see, it will be the same."

"I . . . I daresay it will be, in time!" Charlotte managed to say.

"Well, here now, it's not at all so bad," George continued, awkwardly searching for words of comfort. "I'm sure you'll be much happier with your own people than out jauntering around the countryside after your governess . . ." An awful suspicion came over George and he bent close to the princess, rather roughly removing the hand nearest him from her face.

"And what, may I ask, do you find to laugh at?" he asked awfully. "Here I am trying to offer you all the aid and comfort at my disposal—and believe me, ma'am, it is not at all the line of business that I am used to, not being a courtier—"

"No, no, I am sure it is not! But if you could only know . . ." Charlotte began, not attempting to conceal her amusement any longer. "You have been *bammed*, sir, and bammed very badly! Oh, if you only knew what you have done—"

"What have I done?" George demanded, suddenly looking about him. "Where are we?" he asked, not reasonable at all by this point. "This isn't the Brighton Road! You little hoyden, what sort of trick have you served me now?"

But Charlotte was not paying any attention at all to Lord Ventor, her attention rather suddenly being fixed at some point ahead, her mouth opening into a startled O.

George whipped about to follow her gaze, and beheld, to his utter astonishment, a man mounted upon a horse, swathed up to his eyebrows in a dark cloak, a muffler wrapped about his lower face, standing in the middle of the road, bathed in moonlight. "Stumfundlivah!" this remarkable individual exclaimed as George reined in his weary team.

"I say, you can't sit in the middle of the road and block the progress of travelers!" George called. "Likely to end up in a nasty accident, doing that!"

"Stumfundelivah!" the cloaked horseman repeated, his voice entirely muffled by the scarves wrapped about his jaw.

"What's the fella want? Has he got a toothache?" George asked the princess.

She closed her mouth and swallowed hard. "I think, my lord, he has commanded us to *stand and deliver!*" she exclaimed.

"Just what we need!" George groaned, at the end of his patience. "A highwayman!"

"Oh!" the princess exclaimed, clapping her

hands together. "What excitement! Is he *really* a highwayman?"

"Stumfundelivah!" the man on horseback repeated, and as if to prove his point, withdrew something from the folds of his cloak that glittered rather nastily in the moonlight.

"I . . . I think, my lord, that that *might* be a gun in his hand," Princess Charlotte suggested, gripping at George's coat sleeve uncertainly.

"See here, my good man," George called impatiently, "I've had quite enough trouble for one day, thanks so much."

In reply, the man on horseback pulled the muffler dow from his face, so that a long, lugubrious face was exposed to the moonlight. "What I said was, 'Stand and deliver!' " this remarkable individual said, his tone somewhat aggrieved. "Don't you two know a bird on the toby-lay when you see one? I'm not out here for me health, you know!"

"Indeed, I suppose not," Princess Charlotte agreed. "Night air is injurious to health, after all!"

"An' so it is, miss, although what a bang-up phaeton would be doin' on the Bristol High at such an hour, I don't know! Seems like all respectable sorts of people are at home and in bed! Now, if you'll just step down from that there winged wheeler, an' keep yer hands above yer heads, I won't have to use me popper here!"

"Do as he says," George instructed the princess.

"But why should I?" she asked, fair indignation writ large on her face. "If he wants anything I've got—and believe me, I brought precious little—it seems to me that you ought to at least fight him for it!"

"Don't be foolish!" George implored her.

"Listen to t'gentleman and believe! I'm a dangerous sort of cove when I'm put to the test," advised the highwayman. "An' yer puttin' me to the test, miss!"

"Well, of all shabby things!" the princess muttered, but descended from the phaeton and stood by the side of the road looking up at the man on horseback. "At least one hopes that you do not have to travel too far from here tonight," she said, looking at his big rawboned gelding. "I think your horse is fagged to death."

"And so he is," the highwayman agreed. "It's been a rough week. When I first took to the high toby, I thought it would all be guts and glory, begging your pardon, miss, but I'm here to tell you, it ain't!"

"I shouldn't wonder, if that big spavined creature is the best you can do," Charlotte said sympathetically. "One *reads*, you know, about Dick Turpin's Black Bess, and what a spanking creature *she* was."

The highwayman coughed, his pistol waving about dangerously. "Dick Turpin!" he said with

71

some loathing. "When I took to this lay, I thought I would be like Dick Turpin or Jack Sheppheard or one o' them sorts o' boys! But lemme tell you, it's not half what it's cracked up to be, this business. Half yer nights shivering behind a bush, waiting for innercent travelers to roll by, and when some likely pullet does happen on, ten to one they've so many outriders and postboys that you couldn't get within a mile of them wi'out bein' blown back to hell's north gate, if you'll pardon the expression, miss, and when you do, by chance, find someone ripe for the pluckin', ten to one all you'll end up wid is an ogler or a couple of monkeys for your trouble!" He blew his nose into a large, none-too-clean handkerchief. It was a very large nose, and it made a very loud sound.

"For God's sake, man! We haven't got all night, you know!" George said impatiently. "All I've got is my watch and a couple of guineas, so take it and be damned! It couldn't be any worse than anything else that I've been put to this day!"

The highwayman dabbed at his large proboscis and gave George a woebegone glance. "Ar, what d'you have to complain about? You see what happens when you take up night work? Out in all weathers, and in this sort of a cold snap, like, you're likely to catch cold in more ways than one!"

"Well, the very thing for that, sir, is a hot posset and to be in bed!" the princess said wisely.

"Easy for you to say!" the highwayman replied unhappily. "Like as not, that's just what's waiting for you at the end of your journey! But I'll be lucky if I make enough for a half-pint of bitter and a flop in the doss! It's enough to make a cove turn back to day work!"

"I shouldn't doubt it," the princess replied with a great deal of sympathy, although it was doubtful that she understood above half of what was being said to her, so severe was the highwayman's cold.

"Oh, be quiet, do!" George exclaimed, totally out of patience. "Not only have you plunged me into a world of grief on this day, but you have now ended us up in the clutches of a gallows-bird!"

" 'Ere, now, no need to call names," the highwayman said reprovingly. "Like as not you're not completely clean-sheeted yourself! Fine sort of toff you are, after all, chargin' about the roads in the middle of the night with a female!"

"I say!" George replied. "It lacks only fifteen minutes to the hour . . ." To prove his point, he dug into the vest pocket of his waistcoat, his idea being to remove his watch and look at the time.

But the highwayman must have thought he had other ideas, for there was a flash of light and a thundering bang, and George felt as if he had been slapped on the side of the head, as he went spinning backward. The last thing he heard was the princess's scream echoing in his ears.

6

In later times, Lord Ventor would find that subsequent events were fragmented in his memory, for his wound caused him to pass from consciousness into a feverish nightmare state. He possessed himself of only the vaguest recollections of the anxious faces of the princess and the highwayman standing above him, silvery pale in the moonlight, their voices drifting in and out of his preception.

Dimly, as if from a play he had once seen, he recalled being placed into his phaeton, and the princess shredding a strip of her petticoat and bandaging his head with as much aplomb and *sangfroid* as the most seasoned surgeon, while the highwayman, blowing his nose mournfully, looked on.

"Aspite as things might look, miss, I'm a peaceable sort of cove, and not overgiven to tipping the dubs on anyone, let alone a flash sort of cove who's like as not to be missed," the highwayman said, watching anxiously as she bound up George's wound.

"No more than a graze," she announced.

George roused himself enough to glare at her. "I believe you're enjoying all of this!" he said, and immediately was plunged back into the depths of blackness.

He recalled only dimly a nightmarish voyage over rough and rutted roads, with the princess handling his team with the utmost gentleness, the highwayman riding alongside.

Fragments of their conversation drifted through his mind:

"... do not care how disrespectable a place it may be, as long as he may lay his head somewhere ... not serious, but the shock ..."

"... not in the habit of shooting coves—or morts, for that matter! Sneezed, and me pistol fired off ..."

"... am certain that it was not really your fault ... guns are such deucedly *tricky* things ..."

At one point George opened his eyes to find himself in a small and none-too-clean chamber, stretched out on a bed, while a woman with a number of quivering chins held a lamp close to his head and peered into his face. Over her massive shoulder he vaguely perceived a cast of faces that might have come from the hellish pen of a Cruikshank or from Gillray's

worst excursions into hell, so rough and dissipated were their countenances.

"I say!" George started, only to find one
hand grasped by the princess and the other by
the highwayman.

"Now, be quiet, do!" the princess commanded
calmly. "Ma Grimling is doing her very best
for you!"

"Laudanum's the thing," the massive woman
muttered, and as the highwayman tilted his
head up, the princess held a dirty glass to his
lips and poured a foul-tasting mixture down
his throat, causing him to hack and gag.

"You're poisoning me!" George exclaimed,
and felt himself sinking back into the blackness once again, where a warm and peaceful
haze descended over him as all visions and
nightmares departed, mercifully leaving him
in peace.

"If you was to poison him, Ma," the highwayman said, "all you'd have to do is give him
a drink of the blue ruin you serve here!"

How long he slept, Lord Ventor was never
certain, but it seemed, when he finally rose
into something approaching consciousness once
again, that it must have been for a very long
time, for his eyes had some trouble opening,
his mouth felt as if it were stuffed with cotton
wool, and his head throbbed as if all the devils
of hell were forging their pitchforks in his

skull. Every muscle in his body ached, and to try to sit up and apprehend his surroundings was beyond his powers. Nonetheless, he tried to speak, but all he was capable of emitting was a singular groan.

As his eyes cleared and his mind began to register, however vaguely, his surroundings, he noticed that it was afternoon, for bright sunlight was streaming, as best it could, through a dirty and crack-paned window, and somewhere, not too very far away, a clock was chiming three.

"Ben!" said the princess's voice, very close, "I think he's stirring!"

There was a creak, as if someone had risen from a cane-seated chair, and the unmistakable voice of the highwayman penetrated George's clouded mind. "Aye, that he is, miss, and a good thing, too."

Dimly Princess Charlotte's face began to focus before his eyes, and he noted that she was bending over him with a cloth in her hand. Her blue eyes were dancing and her smile was relieved.

"I am very glad that you are not dead! If you were, it would be above all things awkward, you know!" she cheerfully informed him. "Hold still, now, for I need to dress your wound again."

As she pressed the damp cloth against the side of his head, George winced.

"Spiderwebs and moldy bread! That's the

ticket! I tell you, Ma Grimling's as good as any sawbones!" the highwayman said in a satisfied tone of voice. "Feeling slightly more the thing, are we, soldier?"

George attempted to open his mouth, but for some reason his tongue got in the way, and all he was able to do was give the highwayman a speaking look.

The highwayman's long face, naturally possessed of a mournful expression, took on the look of a wounded beagle dog. "Here, now, solider! No need to look daggers at me! It were an accident, after all, and not done deliberate-like! I sneezed, an' me rozzer blew off! Never let it be said that Ben Stick ever tried to shut anyone's oggles permanent-like!"

"I suppose," George managed to say with some difficulty, "that I am in your debt!" If he had meant his tone to convey all the sarcasm he was feeling, he was not yet in full enough possession of his faculties for his body to follow his brain.

"Yes, we are in Ben's debt, for he has conveyed us to Ma Grimling's, and if it were not for her, you know, you would doubtless be dead right now, for she knew precisely what to do, and how to go about it, which, I assure you, neither Ben nor I did."

"Here, now, I just grazed the side of your head, soldier," Ben said cheerfully. "Laid you into next week, but you'll be all right and tight." The intrinsic cheer of his nature was in such sharp contrast to the lugubriousness of his countenance that George could only stare at him for several seconds, attempting to focus.

Ben Stick was taller than Lord Ventor, and all awkward angles, much exaggerated by his extreme thinness. His mournful face, with his narrow bones and enormous nose above which a pair of speaking brown eyes looked anxiously down at George, resembled, in fact, nothing quite so much as a basset hound wearing a wig of thick brown curls, and his eyebrows, as thick and curly as his hair, almost met at the bridge of his nose. He might have been anywhere between twenty and fifty, with no one the wiser, and as he spoke, he had a nervous habit of pulling at the lobe of one of his jug ears. Under any other set of circumstances George might have found himself liking this rather comical and totally unlikely rescuer, but in his present mood he felt a positive loathing for both Ben Stick and Princess Charlotte.

"Where are we?" he managed to ask, closing his eyes and allowing the princess to wind a bandage about his head.

"We are at the Blood and Feather," Charlotte replied calmly enough, although she could not suppress a giggle as she added, "A not very respectable inn!"

"Hedge tavern!" George moaned. "Oh, my God! What next?"

"Well, I'll admit it's not the sort of place where the quality put up," Ben said, a little offended, "but it'll do for the likes of you! And not a word against Ma Grimling, for she's as *sneck* as they come, and a knowing one into the bargain! No need to worry about anyone peachin' you here, soldier!"

Suddenly the circumstances in which George found himself were borne back upon him and he attempted to sit up. "Good God! We cannot stay here! It's out of the question—"

"Oh, dear, I think he's delirious again," Charlotte said quickly, her fingernails digging into the soft area just below his ear. "Ben, do go and find some more of those opium drops!"

"Aye," Ben said, and George listened to his footsteps as they receded from the room and down a set of stairs.

"That was a close one," Charlotte said, removing her nails from George's neck and giving him a look. "You almost betrayed us, and that would never do, you know!"

"I'll say it would not!" George groaned. "But it's not necessary to claw me to death, either! Good God, look at this place!"

It was, in fact, not a particularly prepossessing chamber. Concealed beneath the eaves, it was obvious that it had been a long time since it had been cleaned and scrubbed out, for dust lay on every flat surface, from the rickety bureau in the corner, one missing leg propped up with bricks, to the sill of the single and very grimy window that looked out over an ill-kempt and muddy stableyard. The quilt beneath which George lay could have stood to be washed and dried in fresh air, and the sheets smelled of pomade from a previous occupant of the bed, which itself was a rickety affair with a lumpy tick. It had been perhaps twenty years since the walls had last been whitewashed, and a three-year-old calendar of the Newmarket Races was their only ornament other than some rudely penciled graffiti on their cracked and yellow surfaces.

As if she were seeing it for the first time, the princess cast a glance about the tiny room. "Well, mine is not much better," she conceded, "and I pushed the bureau up against the door the first night we were here. But that is not the point at all! You must admit that this is a capital sort of adventure, for you cannot imagine the characters I have met in the past few days! So much more interesting than the course of people one generally meets, which is to say, in my case, no one at all!"

"Interesting!" George said bitterly. "Good God, I do not doubt that this is a way-place for every manner of criminal in the West Country!"

"Oh, precisely so! It is most famous! But only consider! Ben could have simply ridden off and left us in the road, you know, and then where would we be? No one would ever think to look for us here!"

Perceiving Charlotte's blue eyes dancing with mischief, George shuddered. "You are *enjoying* this!" he accused her balefully.

"Of course I am," Charlotte replied, totally unruffled. "Only think. At first I *was* a little frightened, you know, but Ma Grimling and Ben immediately depressed anyone's pretensions, and I assure you I am quite safe. Ma, you see, can bend an iron horseshoe out straight with two hands, and everyone is in awe of her!"

"Good Lord," George said, and became totally nonplussed.

"Well, anyway, you shall meet her soon and thank her for saving your life, for she did so, you know, but I think you ought to know that I decided that it might be best if we did not appraise anyone else of our true identities—it might lead to *complications*, you see," the princess explained naively. "So I told everyone that you and I had contracted an engagement of which my family did not approve, and that we were running away to be married! I gave my name as Miss Prince. Was that not ingenious?"

George opened and closed his mouth, his eyebrows rising up to his forehead in a manner that would have done credit to Phipps, but he found himself incapable of doing other than listening to the fantastic tale the princess had concocted from plain air.

"I said that I am an heiress and that you are a very brave soldier—well, you were, were you not? And that our engagement had been one of long standing, but when you came back from the wars to claim my hand, my father had contracted me to marry an odious man named Ramplesham—do not look at me so, I would very much like to see you concoct a likely tale on your feet in just as fast a manner as I did!—and that I had been locked in my room until I agreed! But you climbed up the trellis outside my window and released me, and we came away instantly, and were on our way to book passage for a ship to America when Ben laid upon us. Was it not a good sort of a runner?"

In spite of himself, George had to chuckle. "One can only hope our hosts are not avid readers of novels!" he said dryly.

"I daresay it would make a very good novel," the princess replied sanguinely. "But all you must do is agree to everything I have said. You see, the penalty for kidnapping heiresses to marry is transportation to the antipodes, so now they all think you are a hedge bird, just like they are!"

"If I am not beheaded for treason first,"

George sighed, shaking his head. "Do you know what sort of a hue and cry must be up after you by this time? Even here, they must read newspapers, must hear the news!"

Princess Charlotte gurgled with laughter as she produced an old and wrinkled newspaper. "Among such other interesting things as Queen Charlotte attending church at St. Hilda's at Windsor, and Lady Cappel succeeding Lady Norwich as lady-in-waiting, it says that her royal highness the Princess Charlotte is taking the waters in Weymouth, where she is together with her retinue aboard one of the royal yachts! So, you see, I am not really here at all! Oh, I should have loved to see their faces, those old dragons, when they found I had given them the slip!"

"Thieves' cant sits ill on the lips of the Princess of Wales," George reminded her rather stuffily.

"Oh, bosh!" Charlotte replied, folding the paper and casting it aside. "Every buck in London has a far greater command of cant than anyone I have met here so far! But you see, Papa is covering up for me! Doubtless he thinks I have run off to find my mother in Italy, although nothing, I assure you, would be less likely!"

Not anxious to involve himself in royal domestic quarrels, George only shook his head. "Lord, what a tangle!" he sighed.

Charlotte sighed. "I think you are a very poor sort of companion for an adventure. I would imagine that Prince Leopold would fall right into the spirit of things!"

"I imagine Prince Leopold would feel as I do, that things are entirely out of control, and the sooner I remove you from this place, the better it will be for all of us! It doesn't seem to occur to you that we are in danger!"

The blue eyes surveyed him. Charlotte's understanding was not profound, but neither was she a fool. "But, my lord, in the meantime it behooves us to make the best of the situation we find ourselves in," she said calmly. Then the mischief danced in her eyes again. "Besides, only wait until you meet Ribbon Peg, and Red-Eye Jack, and the rest! I assure you, they are bang-up folk!"

"You stay in your room!" George commanded. With more strength than he had, he attempted to sit up, but the effort proved too great for his weakened condition, and he collapsed, dizzy and light-headed, back against the evil pillow.

"There, now!" the princess exclaimed. "You see what happened when you tried to overexert yourself? I promise you, I shall behave appropriately, but the important thing, my lord, is that you rest and repair yourself!"

At that moment Ben Stick appeared in the doorway again, bearing a blue bottle and a glass, and no more was said about their circumstance.

George's head throbbed so badly that he made no demur when the princess mixed several drops of the tincture into water and bade him drink it.

Before very long, he was asleep again, to dream uneasy dreams.

7

When next George awakened, it was night-fall, for the room was dark, and only a single tallow candle smoked and burned fitfully on the bureau, casting a dim and shadowing light over the tiny room.

His head had cleared slightly, and with only a very little effort he was able to sit up in bed, rubbing his eyes with the heels of his hands and feeling gingerly at the bandage about his head, which he was pleased to find no longer throbbed and ached with dancing demons.

From downstairs there was the sound of merriment and laughter, and although he could not make out the words, he could hear that an accordion was being played and a song being sung in a slurred female voice. Looking about the room, he apprehended that he was alone, and he was suddenly filled with concern for Princess Charlotte.

His clothes lay neatly folded over the back of a rump-sprung cane chair, and gingerly George swung his feet out of bed and placed them on the cold and dusty floor. For a moment his head swam, and he had to draw several deep breaths before he felt he could stand on his feet.

His experience with wounds in Spain prepared him for the sudden weakness he felt when he managed to stand up, grappling at the bedpost for support, and he patiently supported himself until he felt the circulation restoring itself to his legs and feet before he peeled off the coarse linen nightshirt someone (Ben Stick? Ma Grimling? *Not*, he hoped, Princess Charlotte!) had dressed him in and began to pull on his breeches and his stockings.

His coat proved too great an effort, and there was no mirror to tell him how he looked, but George was pleased to find that his door was not locked, and carefully, feeling along the walls, he stumbled down the narrow stairs in the darkness, suspicious of what he might find there and wary of possible guards lurking in the dark.

However, he made his way down to the first floor without impediment, and stood in the open doorway of the brightly lit taproom, blinking in the sudden illumination as he took in the scene before his eyes, unbelieving of what he saw.

So loud and merry were the ill-assorted revelers in that room that he might have driven a coach and four down the hall without notice. Like the rest of the Blood and Feathers, it was shabby and run-down, and desperately in need of a good scouring.

Smoke belched forth from the huge stone chimneyhearth against the far wall, and the exposed beams and plastered walls were gray with smoke and age. Tallow candles stood in braces on the wall, the wax long ago having obscured the sconces beneath formless puddles, and sawdust had been scattered on the floor to absorb the spilled beer and debris beneath the feet of this unholy-looking company. On a spit over the blazing fire, an enormous haunch of a doubtless poached deer was being turned by a slatternly maid whose dubious charms were exposed to the world by a stained muslin dress that was cut far too deep at the bosom and far too short in the hem. A vulpine boy somewhere in mid-adolescence, to judge by the outbreak of spots on his sallow complexion, was filling mugs from a cask of no doubt smuggled Hollands as fast as he could, for the patrons of the Blood and Feather were a thirsty lot.

And what a lot they were! Again George had the feeling that he had stepped into one of the more grotesque offerings of Cruikshank or Gillray, for only that pair of wicked caricaturists could have created such a gathering of humanity.

To begin with, there was the woman whom he recognized to be Ma Grimling herself, an enormous female spilling out from all directions upon the chair in which she sat, knees apart, hands on her huge thighs, stockings spilling out over her shoes and the flesh of her ankles spilling out above that, raising her gintenor in an old and decidedly lewd drinking song. A ruffled cap concealed most of her unlikely blond hair, and rouge bloomed across her vast cheeks like overblown roses. Her small, sharp eyes were concealed behind a pair of scholarly-looking wire spectacles, which perched upon her beak of a nose in a most precarious fashion. As she sang, all of her many chins quivered, along with the lacy fichu that covered her vast bosom. Attired in a dress of pink and white silk bombazine, she resembled nothing so much as a sack made from a wedding tent. One look at her enormous upper arms convinced George that she could indeed bend a horseshoe, if so inclined, for her bulk contained equal proportions of fat and muscle.

At her side, half-sprawled across the table behind his chair, sat a man dressed all in shiny black, with the look of a cleric about his pale, drawn face, save for the black eyepatch that concealed his left eye. No cleric that George knew of would frequent such a low place, nor would he ply an accordion in such an enthusiastic way, from time to time lifting his voice in the chorus of the song.

Taking his ease in a chair beside the fire, a mug in his hand, sat Ben Stick, clearly more than a little drunk, tapping his worn boot against the sawdust in time to the music, looking for all the world as if he were at a wake rather than a party.

But what truly stunned George was the sight of Princess Charlotte in the middle of the room, walking slowly back and forth before a tailor's dummy attired in a coat whose pockets and sleeves were sewn with small bells. As she would pass, she appeared to be pushing her hands into the pockets of this strange coat in order to extract bits of cloth. As she did so, the small bells jingled faintly, and she made a face.

"That's the spirit!" Ma Grimling interrupted her song to cry loudly, stamping her feet against the floor and accepting the mug proffered by the boy at the tap. "The bells jingled only a little that time! We'll soon have you kenny to the dipping-lay, my girl!"

"Charlotte!" George exclaimed in a horrible voice from the doorway, and instantly the room fell silent as all faces turned toward him. "Picking pockets?" George demanded awfully.

Charlotte flushed, and looked very sulky indeed, but Ben Stick, in an effort to smooth over a possibly awkward social situation, stood unsteadily upon his feet. "Just a little family party, soldier," he said in a slurred voice.

"A little—" George began to say, and was silenced by the sight of Ma Grimling rising to her feet. Even from across the room he could see that she was as tall as he, but there was something compelling in the way she shifted her bulk across the floor toward him, rather like a laden-down man-o'-war under full sail, and clapped him heartily across the shoulder.

"Well, soldier," she boomed in her gin-tenor voice, coarse and gravelly, "good to see you back on your feet! Red-Eye, fetch the man a mug of this good Hollands! I'm Ma Grimling, and this is my inn."

"H-how do you do?" George stammered, overwhelmed as much by her person as by the blast of gin on her breath.

"I do just fine, but it's you we were all worrit about, soldier! Like as not thought the brain fever would carry you off!"

Recovering himself slightly, George murmured that he understood his healing was entirely her work, and that he owed her a great deal of thanks, a remark that Ma Grimling brushed off with a shrug.

"Be that as if may, it's no good to have the paying guests turning up their toes! This ain't the sort of place where we want a great deal of attention from certain quarters, if you get my meaning."

George did, but before he had to make any reply, the little cleric with the eyepatch was handing him a mug. "This will set your bones," he promised in a high-pitched voice.

"Soldier, my better half, Red-Eye Jack!" boomed Ma Grimling, gazing several inches down and with great fondness at her clerical spouse, who gazed back up at his enormous wife with equal adoration.

"Glad to see you up and about, hey?" Red-Eye Jack piped. "Ma can pull *anyone* through," he added.

"And lay 'em away, too, if I've a mind," Mrs. Grimling boomed jovially. "That there's my girl, Ribbon Peg, over there turning the spit, and my son, Blue Ruin, although we mostly call him Blue, on account of his pa and I made him one night on the Blue Ruin!"

George nodded to these two individuals, who returned his nod with their own. Neither one seemed to be possessed of any great understanding, or perhaps they were too far gone in celebration to be more forthcoming.

"Just a little family gathering," Ben Stick repeated, standing up to give George his place by the fire.

George was grateful to sink into a seat, and, slightly stunned, he looked about himself, wondering what diabolical twist of fate had landed him among these characters.

Ben had set about carving off a great hunk of venison from the roast on the spit, and from the coals withdrew a couple of baked potatoes, all of which he placed upon a plate and handed to George.

"Eat up, my lad, blood makes blood," he advised, and George, suddenly discovering his appetite, did as he was bid. The venison was surprisingly delicious.

Mrs. Grimling settled herself back into her seat opposite him and watched him eat with satisfaction. "It's just as Ben says, soldier! Blood makes blood, and I don't doubt that with a hearty meal or two, you'll be all the thing again!"

"The sooner the better, ma'am," George said politely, as Ribbon Peg leaned over him to hand him a stained muslin napkin, and in the process revealed a great deal more of her charms than George really wanted to see. She smiled at him, revealing very poor teeth. "I do not doubt that you are as anxious to see the last of the . . . of Miss Prince and myself as we are to continue on our way!"

Ma Grimling's shrewd little eyes raked over him from behind her glasses, and her several chins bobbed in agreement. "Miss has told us something of your circumstance, soldier, but you've come to a place where it's best to tell as little as you can and ask few questions of others, if you get my meaning."

George nodded. "I think I do," he said. "But as you can see, Miss Prince and I are in a tangle of our own."

He glanced at Charlotte, who had taken a seat beside him, her lips quivering dangerously as she inquired, "My darling, do you feel quite as if you ought to be out of bed yet?"

"I'm settled," he remarked. "But it's you I'm worried about ... *my love!*" he remembered to add.

Ben Stick, having refreshed his glass, lowered himself a little unsteadily into a chair he turned back to front. Leaning on the backrest, he gazed rather plaintively at George. "Well, again, soldier, I'm right sorry I winged you there, but it couldn't be helped. I sneezed, you know, and the blasted pistol went off. I should have known better than to go on the High Toby with a hair-trigger gun!" He shook his head and looked so mournful that George laughed, the Hollands coursing in his system and mellowing him considerably.

"It's all of a piece, believe me!" he said firmly. "From start to finish, this adventure has been fraught with mishap!"

Charlotte shook her head. "Truly, we have had a sad tangle!" she sighed. "But now we are among friends, so all may turn out right yet!"

George did not see quite how, but he said nothing, only frowned at the princess in a rather unloverlike way.

"Ah, now, you mustn't take it so hard that we was putting her in the way of learning how to dip," Red-Eye Jack said, patting his wife's hand. "She was bored, you see, and Ma's a great one to pass on what she knows."

"I ran the best dipping school in London before we retired and became respectable," Mrs. Grimling agreed. "No one can say Ma Grimling's but generous when it comes to spreading her knowledge out among the younger generation."

"If by that you mean you ran a school for pickpockets," George said, "I can well believe that you were an excellent preceptress. It is just that I do not feel that Miss Prince should pick up any more bad habits than those she is already possessed of!"

Charlotte's eyelashes fluttered demurely. "Well, my love, you never know when such a talent will be most useful in my ... in our future life!"

"Mark on, she's being taught by the best, soldier!" Ben added. "Why, Ma could relieve a judge of his wig on the bench and no one the wiser, she was that good in her time!"

"I have no doubt of that," George said sincerely.

"Here, now," Ma said, rising and shaking out her voluminous skirts. "No nabbling on about the past! Me'n Jack are set up respectable now ... well, almost respectable, except for that hedge bird there, and why we keep him among us, I'll never know, save Ben's like family to us, so there's no use us falling hipped over old times!"

"How right you are, Ma, my dear!" Red-Eye Jack proclaimed fondly. "It was always our dream, you know, to purchase just such a place as this, quiet and tucked away in the country, where we might escape the hustle and bustle of city life!"

Picking up a poker, Mrs. Grimling stirred up a log in the fire. "Not," she grunted, "that one doesn't sometimes miss the city, and all of one's friends, but things were just of a piece, you see! 'Always leave the table on a winning streak' has been my motto, and so here you see us, as snug as can be!"

"Very commendable!" George said dryly. "But trade does not seem as brisk as it might be."

"Ain't it the truth!" Ma Grimling sighed, readjusting herself to her chair. "Well, there you have it, and no doubt! It always takes time for customers to establish themselves to new management, and this is an out-of-the-way sort of district, where the locals distrust city folk! But we get by, we get by!"

George, looking about himself, could have made a few suggestions that might have increased honest business, but wisely kept his tongue between his teeth, having no doubt that the sort of clientele the Grimlings encouraged were persons who for one reason or another found it wise to remove themselves from their usual haunts until such time as the hue and cry engendered by their activities had died down.

"Well, now, we've told you a great deal more than you need to know, soldier," Ben Stick said, looking at George out of the corner of his eye. "But it would seem that you're up to your ears in an entanglement of your own, so doubtless you'll stow your gab!"

"You may depend upon us," Charlotte said a little breathlessly, putting a hand over George's. "Certainly no one else would have shown us the kindness that you have!" she added passionately.

Mrs. Grimling nodded, chins aquiver as she beamed fondly upon Charlotte. "Well, now, miss, I suppose it's because we've all taken a liking to you. Poor thing!" she added, looking at George and shaking her head sadly. "The trials she's been through, it's enough to soften the devil's own soul. "As if it weren't bad enough that her father sent her poor ma away when a girl's of the age to be needin' a mother the most, but to lock her in a room and put her on bread and water because she won't marry a limping old man who could be her grandpa an's already buried three wives under what seem to me to be havey-cavey circumstances, all for the sake of a title!"

George cast a look at the princess, who wisely dropped her eyes to her hands, demurely folded in her lap, and sighed pitifully. "Papa beat me!" she said in a low voice. "With a horsewhip!"

"Y'poor t'ing!" exclaimed Ribbon Peg, much moved. "Why t'only thing Ma ever raised to me was the back of her hand, and that when I lost me head and tipped the dibbs on the Redbreasts—"

"And you deserved it, too, you silly girl!" Red-Eye Jack admonished her. "Only fancy, there we were with seven gold watches and dunno how many rings and bracelets to fence up, and Peg would lose her head when Bow Street was at the door."

"No use cryin' over spilt milk," said Blue from behind the tap, scratching at his spots. "I gave 'em the run, didn't I just?"

"Be that as it may," Mrs. Grimling said repressively, obviously not anxious to discuss the family's erstwhile fortunes in front of strangers. "Lord, soldier, you're a bloody hero, *I* says! Imagine, comin' home from the wars, all decorated up with medals, and finding your sweetheart's father had cheated you out of every cent of your poor parents' money that they died and left you to start a new life! Ah, the blackest villains aren't the likes of the Seven Dials, they're the ones with the pen and paper that like to rob you the most!" She clucked her tongue.

"It . . . it was most difficult, ma'am!" George said unsteadily.

"Imagine, though," Blue offered, "you showed him what was what when you fought with rapiers on the staircase, right?"

"Absolutely right!" George agreed rashly. "Although I am certain that my . . . intended greatly exaggerates my exploits! She is prone to hero worship, I fear!"

"Well, I think you are quite the hero!" Ribbon Peg sighed admiringly, looking at George with sheep's eyes. "If a cove come along an' rescued me from a house my father had set fire to in order to shut me up against all his dreadful crimes, I should think him a proper sort of cove!"

George choked on his Hollands, and it was several moments before he trusted himself to speak again. "Doing it a bit too brown!" he murmured under the guise of affectionately kissing the top of Charlotte's head. To the rest of the company, obviously enthralled with the princess's banbury tale, he smiled in a self-deprecatory manner. "I love my, er . . . fiancée dearer than my own life," he managed to say, attempting to keep his tone casual, "but I am not blind to her chief character fault, which is to be so besotted in love that she perceives me as a pattern card of all virtue and bravery, and tends to exaggerate my exploits a great deal more than is absolutely necessary. Is that not correct, my love?"

Charlotte wrinkled her nose, but managed to look at him adoringly. "Oh, that is true," she breathed in tones that would have done credit to Mrs. Siddons. "I fear that such is my regard for my dear, dear George that I wish all the world to see him as I do!" As she took his hand into her own, her fingernails dug into the palm of his hand in a decidedly unladylike way, but George only returned her the blandest of smiles.

From a pocket Ben Stick withdrew a large spotted handkerchief that he had obviously relieved from some member of the Four Horse Club and blew his nose. "There ain't *nothing* like true love," he said a little soddenly.

"No, there ain't," Mrs. Grimling said, and her shrewd small eyes met George's just for a second in such a way that he wondered if Charlotte had overplayed her hand in such a way as to cast them both into deep danger. But the flash was gone as soon as it had come, her large face wreathed in smiles. "Well," she said, rising again from her chair and shaking out her skirts, "I'd daresay from the look of our soldier boy here that he's fagged to death just by coming down the stairs and havin' to sit in company with us, and that won't do! Miss, you and Ben sneck him away up the stairs now, and we'll all turn in for the evening."

"My horses—" George started to say.

"Stabled up right and tight, soldier, and prime cattle they are, too! Look after 'em myself! You've given them the devil's own ride, and your left leader's sore in the fetlock, but happen I'll set that all right and tight, so don't tease yourself!"

"Pray do not!" Charlotte agreed, helping Ben to assist George to stand. "Ben Stick is an excellent man with horses!"

"Nay, soldier, rest tranquil! You've naught to worry about from us as long as you're at the Blood and Feather!" Mrs. Grimling promised him, folding her huge arms across her waist, or rather the place where her waist should have been. Again she gave him that shrewd look. "Quality or not, I can promise you that we won't squeak beef upon you here for miss's sake!"

Before George could ponder her meaning, Charlotte and Ben Stick had drawn him out the taproom door and up the stairs again, where he was glad enough to sink into his rusty sheets and a dreamless slumber.

8

George's strength did not return to him as fast as he thought it should, and he spent several more days in bed, restless and fretful to be up and on his way again. However, each time Ben Stick dressed him, it was all he could do to sit in the chair by the window for a few hours each day, watching the autumnal landscape plunge into gold-and-orange fire.

Nor was his healing in any way aided by the princess, for whom he felt a distinct responsibility and an increasing uneasiness. Although she played the role of nurse to Mrs. Grimling's doctor with an unexpected dispatch, and seemed in every way suited to the extremely odd circumstances of her situation, George could not help but fret, when she was out of his sight, that she was up to some prank or other that might endanger not only their disguise but also her own life.

The princess had been kept too long on short tether and sheltered from far too many of the day-to-day realities that even the most well-brought-up girls of her own age could deal with simply and routinely so, her natural high spirits and hoydenish personality, allowed to progress unchecked, could only, George felt, lead to the most disastrous of consequences, and as a result, he was so full of commands and maxims toward her that she, not unnaturally, began to chafe at his lectures, and informed him that he was not her governess.

"No," George replied peevishly, "and I thank God that I am not!"

"Believe me, my lord," Charlotte informed him as she plumped his pillows and served him his meals on a tray, "far more scandal-broth brews at Brighton than in the Blood and Feather at present! Mrs. Grimling has Peg sleeping in my room as a sort of chaperon, if you will, and her snoring drives me to distraction! When I am not here with you, I am out with Ben Stick seeing to the horses, and no persons of quality could have been more civil hosts to me than the Grimlings!"

"I trust you are learning to pick pockets to admiration," George countered bitterly, and received a royal stare for his pains, as Charlotte placed a tray of cold ham and bread on his lap.

"Well," she said, "you never know when

such a talent might come in handy in my future life, do you?" Her eyes were so full of bland innocence that George could only shake his head, for there was some wisdom to what she said, however cracked her logic might be. "Anyway, this is a capital adventure, is it not?" she continued, cutting his meat for him. "Only fancy, I almost had Ben persuaded last night to let me ride the High Toby with him! I would dress as a boy, of course—you have no idea of the trunks and trunks of secondhand clothes Ma Grimling has, from her old days as a fence—a receiver of stolen goods, you know! Well, Peg and I picked out some boy's clothes and outfitted me, and with my hair pulled up beneath a hat, you would not know me from a boy! When I walked into the taproom, Blue thought I was a stranger! The *look* on his face! Of course, you know, Ben thinks that I am a ripping horsewoman and would make quite a good hedge-bird, and I've *almost* won him over to the idea, only of course Mrs. Grimling would not like it at all—but can you imagine the look on my dear papa's face if he should find out his daughter was relieving cits of their rings and watches?" Charlotte chortled.

As George hoisted himself out of bed, plate, ham, and bread went flying across the room, and the princess nearly lost her balance on the chair she had been perching upon.

"I say!" she exclaimed as George threw the

window sash up and thrust his head out into the air above the stableyard, where Ben was whistling between his teeth as he groomed his gelding.

"Ben! Get up here!" George roared. "At once, I say!"

What followed was a rare scene indeed, as George read the highwayman a strongly phrased lecture about the inadvisability of allowing gently nurtured young ladies of an impressionable age to take it into their heads to play at being highwaymen.

Contrite, Ben Stick was quick to defend himself by saying that it was only a lark, and he had no intention of allowing Miss to risk life and limb in a lay that was dangerous enough for those who were born to the profession such as himself, let alone allowing a regular green 'un such as Miss to attempt the dangers of the High Toby, aside from which she could not hit the broad side of a barn door with a pistol at two paces and, in times of duress, tended to act flighty rather than keeping a cool head as was needed for such enterprises.

These remarks disparaging her character as a brigand, the princess not unnaturally took with very bad grace indeed, insisting that she was in every way suitable to the profession she had chosen, pointing out that *she* was not such a maw-worn as to pass up a perfectly good barouche with only a groom, a coachman, and one outrider like *some* persons she knew, who were chickenhearted in the extreme, and no wonder.

When both George and Ben Stick pointed out the unsuitability of a young lady attempting any such prank at all, and particularly in their circumstances, Charlotte was brought to see a certain degree of reason, but the entire episode left George exhausted and full of the headache, Ben Stick walking about muttering morosely to himself, and Charlotte locked into her room with a fit of the sulks that lasted all day.

It was the dinner hour when an uncharacteristically gloomy Ben thrust his head around the door of George's room. "Are you awake, soldier?" he asked, sniffling. "I've brought up your dinner. Miss don't want any, and Peg made an apple cobbler for her especially."

Knowing all too well that the special culinary talents of Peg included an ability to cook everything so that it tasted like leather, George was not surprised that the princess could resist this treat. However, he beckoned Ben into the room, bidding him to shut the door behind him and have a seat.

Ben, sensing that he might be about to be absolved of his offenses, did as he was bid, setting the tray upon the table and folding his gangling legs beneath the rungs of the chair, looking at George with large, trusting basset-hound eyes.

"Look," George said abruptly, sitting up in bed with difficulty. "I've been thinking, Ben."

Ben inclined his head to one side, listening.

George ran his hand over his bandage. "I've been lying here all afternoon, worrying about Miss Prince. She's a high-strung girl, you know."

"That she is, and more," Ben agreed. "A regular hoyden, that one can be."

George nodded. "Well, she is that and all, I'll be the first to admit, and the hell of it is, Ben, I'm powerless to check her, laid up here as I am."

"It's a rum situation, all right," Ben agreed sympathetically. "Miss is like as not broke to bridle, but she's like a nag that's been penned up in its stall yon long and just let out to pasture. Likes to kick up her heels."

"Exactly so!" George agreed, glad that Ben saw things in his way. "Well, the thing of it is, I think she needs someone here to keep an eye on her, keep her from her worst scrapes. If it's not the High Toby, God only knows what start she'll take into her head next!"

Ben nodded sympathetically, but became slightly wary, as if he expected what was to come next, and how it would inevitably involve him.

"I've cast about and cast about, and you see,

this isn't one of those situations where you can ask just any friend to come and bail you out of the suds. It takes a very special sort of person, Ben, and I want you to take a note to her."

"*Her*?" Ben repeated, slightly incredulous.

"*Her*," George repeated. "Her name is Elizabeth Webster, and she lives at Ventor Cross. Her father's the rector there."

"Snab me!" Ben exclaimed. "This ain't precisely the sort of place I'd invite a dominie's daughter!"

"Under ordinary circumstances, neither would I," George admitted. "But these are hardly ordinary circumstances! Will you ride over there and fetch her back? You may take my phaeton! But, Ben, discretion is necessary—get me pen and paper and I'll write her a note explaining all of it, and tell you how you must reach her!"

When he heard the wheels of his phaeton rolling out of the stableyard, George fell back against the pillows and closed his eyes, exhausted.

Clearly, help was needed, but after his experience with Lady Serena Ramplesham, Lord Ventor was understandably reluctant to embroil any of his friends in this particular tangle in which he found himself. Several times in the course of the afternoon Elizabeth Webster had come to his mind, and several times he had rejected the idea out of hand. This was not the sort of affair in which he wished to involve not just a female, but one of his oldest and most trusted friends. Aside from those considerations, he was reluctant to allow Elizabeth to find him in his present circumstances, for there was nothing to appeal to him in allowing her to know what a perfect fool he had made of himself, particularly with Lady Serene Ramplesham. *Why* he should feel an aversion to allowing Miss Webster to know the details of that particular episode in his life, he was uncertain. But in the end he knew that Elizabeth was the one person upon whom he could depend totally, and with the welfare of the princess to consider as well as his own, there seemed to be no person of his wide circle of friends who would be able to deal as discreetly and efficiently with the matter as Miss Webster.

Secure that he had made the right decision, George drifted off to sleep.

9

It was, again, a Friday at the rectory, and the manse was silent except for the occasional bursts of phrase from the locked door of the rector's study. Since he had chosen Deuteronomy 24:19 as his text, there was a great deal about bread and charity and crying over spilt milk, but Elizabeth, who had long ago learned to ignore whatever she might hear from the rector's study when he was in the throes of his sermon, paid no attention.

Once she looked up from *Mansfield Park* and allowed her glance to stray toward the open French doors, as if she expected to see a familiar figure striding across the threshold, and if her expression was a trifle wistful, there was no one to witness it. With a small shake of her head, as if to dismiss vain thoughts, she returned to her reading and was soon lost again in the doings of Miss Austen's delightful characters.

In fact, she had become so engrossed in her reading that she did not see the lanky figure appearing over the edge of the terrace and looking anxiously about, as if expecting to be called to order at any moment, before scratching at the windowpane and hissing.

From the outset, Ben Stick had had his doubts about the wisdom of this enterprise, and the sight of a young lady seated in a wing chair reading while a pair of dogs dozed at her feet was not calculated to inspire his confidence in a happy outcome.

But he clawed again at the window and hissed, and this time one of the dogs gave a warning bark and lazily ambled across the room to investigate.

The young lady looked up, and if her expression was a trifle disappointed, at least she registered no surprise, merely rising from the chair, laying the thin book aside, and crossing the floor to unlatch the door. "Yes," she said in a calm, pleasant voice. "May I help you?"

The bitch had joined her mate, and was interestedly sniffing about Ben's shabby boots, but since both dogs were wagging their tails in a friendly way, Ben took heart and withdrew George's letter from his breast pocket, handing it to Miss Webster, for certainly she fit the description George had given him.

Miss Webster studied the handwriting for a minute, then glanced anxiously at Ben Stick. "He is all right?" she asked softly.

Ben tugged at his ear. "Well, he could be worse," he admitted. "Best you read what he's wrote, ma'am."

Elizabeth broke the seal and did so, her expression changing from one of mild anxiety to deepest puzzlement before her lips curved upward in gentle amusement. She looked at Ben Stick. "Come in, Mr. Stick," she said, stepping back to allow him to enter. "It will take me only a few minutes to be ready. In the meantime, you may go down to the kitchen, down that hall to your left, and ask Cook to fix you something to eat. Tell her you've come about a sick parishioner." She smiled again, and Ben was pleased to note there was a twinkle in her eyes. "It is not precisely a falsehood, you know," she added as she walked him to the doorway and pointed down the hall toward the kitchen.

Ben fully expected that he would be marooned in the kitchen beneath the curious stare of the cook for at least an hour, but he was just finishing off a mutton pie when Miss Webster appeared in the doorway carrying a small valise and wearing a traveling coat and hat over her bottle-green kerseymere round gown.

"Mr. Stick has come to fetch me to a sick parishioner over in Ottery St. Mary's," she announced to Cook. "I will probably not return in time for Sunday services, but I have left the rector a note which he will probably not see, so please tell him where I've gone. I am ready, Mr. Stick."

"My question is, is the Blood and Feather ready for you?" Ben Stick asked himself as he followed Miss Webster down the hall.

If Miss Webster was discomfited by the ramshackle exterior of the Blood and Feather, in the fine light of day even more decrepit and forlorn than it had been the night Ben Stick brought his two erstwhile victims there to sanctuary, she gave no indication.

"Mind, I'm sure it's not what a lady like you is accustomed to, Miss Webster," Ben said apologetically as he handed her down from the phaeton. "Bein' a rector's daughter an' all, and accustomed, no doubt, to quality ways."

Elizabeth, with only a single glance to spare for the peeling sign hanging by one chain beside the threshold, depicting a feather dripping gore, neither fell into the hysterics that Ben half-expected nor demanded that he deliver her safely back to the rectory at once. "Well, I daresay it could do with a coat of whitewash," she admitted in what could possibly have been the greatest understatement she would ever make in her life, but she was in no way deterred from picking up her valise and stepping over the crumbling brick stoop into the inn.

"I think it best if you take, er ... the major's team around to the stables, Mr. Stick, and I shall make myself known to your Mrs. Grimling at once," she commanded calmly, and Ben, after due thought, allowed as how this quiet, self-possessed young woman might know best.

In a very short time Miss Webster was up the stairs and knocking upon the door of Lord Ventor's chamber.

If she was dismayed by the sight of her old friend looking very much the worse for wear, with a bandage wrapped about his head and a not-too-clean rough linen nightshirt covering his body as he sat weakly in a shabby armchair beside the window with an ancient copy of the *Turf Remembrancer* as his only entertainment, she did not betray it, only suppressed a gurgle of laughter as he lifted a woebegone face to her entrance.

"Well, there he sits, Miss Webster, and if there's aught you can do for him, you have but to call," Mrs. Grimling said behind her, clearly upon good terms with this third unexpected guest at the Blood and Feather.

"Thank you, Mrs. Grimling!" Elizabeth said in her calm voice. "I think eventually we shall have to turn this room out and wash the sheets, but for the moment all I require is some privacy with Lo ... with the major. He has a great deal of explaining to do."

"That and all," Mrs. Grimling agreed, shutting the door and shuffling down the hallway in her down-at-heel mules.

Lord Ventor attempted to rise, but Elizabeth ruthlessly pressed him back into his chair.

"Lizzie! By all that's wonderful, I knew you would not let me down!" George exclaimed. "I have never been so glad to see anyone in my entire life as you! Forgive me for dragging you into this hellhole, but I could think of no other person upon whom I could call for aid!"

Miss Webster, untying the strings of her bonnet and dropping it on top of the bureau, where it raised a cloud of dust, shook her head, unable to control the laughter that rose to her lips. "Oh, George, whatever pelter have you landed yourself in here? I might expect to find Trevor laid up in a hedge tavern, but *never* commonsensical, prosaic George!"

As she spoke, she opened her valise and began to lay out an assortment of bandages, scissors, powders, and medicines, ignoring the dust that clung to the hems of her skirts.

"Oh, Lizzie, it's a long story. I assume you received my note, or you would not be here at all."

"Yes, and what an excessively mysterious note it was! I am not to refer to you by your title, but as Major, and your companion is a Miss Prince? Dear me, don't tell me you are eloping with Lady Serena? And Mr. Stick—such a very diverting man! Do hold still while I change that bandage. I apprehend Mr. Stick *shot* you?"

Now that Elizabeth was there, George suddenly felt that he could relax at last, and he leaned back in the chair and closed his eyes as Elizabeth's cool and expert fingers tended to his wound.

With as little roundaboutation as a field report, George gave Miss Webster an account of all of his adventures of the past week, expecting at several points that she would either claim he was mad or exclaim in disbelief that anyone so generally staid as Lord Ventor could give in to such follies. Since he punctuated the tale with self-recriminations of an extremely harsh nature, from time to time Elizabeth did shake her head and cluck her tongue, but it was not until he had finished that she stood back and critically examined her own handiwork, nodded approval of his new dressing, and sat down on the edge of the unmade bed, regarding him with amusement and shaking her head from side to side.

"Well, *you* may laugh," George said defensively, "but I'm in the devil's own mess!"

Elizabeth bit her lower lip. "Forgive me, George! You of all people should know that my worst sin is my most deplorable sense of humor! But you are quite right—it is a fantastic tale! And you say that this is the Princess of

Wales? Oh, I should have given anything to see Serena Ramplesham's face!"

"You're talking about the woman I intended to make my wife!" George exclaimed sulkily. "I ain't proud of it, that's certain! I doubt she'll ever listen to any explanation again!"

Elizabeth's eyes dropped to her hands, folded in her lap. "Very likely not," she said quietly. "I *am* sorry, George."

"Not half as sorry as I am! Very likely she's circulated the story throughout Bath that I've run mad, and no wonder. Indeed, I *must* be mad, to have embroiled myself in this scheme!"

Elizabeth shook her head. "No, I think you acted as any gentleman would have done. It was right and noble and brave of you, George. And quite romantic!"

"Do you think so, Lizzie?" Lord Ventor asked, a little flattered by her good opinion.

"Indeed I do," Miss Webster agreed heartily, two faint spots of color appearing in her cheeks as she arose and threw open the window to allow some fresh air into the room. "I think," she said in a more practical tone, "that it would be best if you were to rest here until you are well enough to travel. To be jauntering about the country under these circumstances would surely lead to a greater scandal, anyway. But I think that I might go and make myself known to her royal highness. We can make no decisions about the future without consulting her, I think."

"If she has her way, she'll either be hanged as a highwayman or run off to tread the boards in a breeches part!" George said bitterly. "A more caper-witted, headstrong creature I have yet to encounter!"

Elizabeth shook her head, sighing. "Well, I shall go and see if she will talk to *me*, at least. Perhaps I can coax her out of her sullens with a woman's touch."

"Good luck!" George said.

She rose and walked toward the door. Suddenly, her hand on the knob, she halted, her shoulders shaking. Slowly she turned about to look at him, her face full of amusement. "Of all the people in the world to tangle himself into running away with the Princess of Wales, only to find himself in a den of the most ... well, improbable persons, George, *you* would never have been my first candidate!"

She gave him a long look, but before George could think of a reply, she was gone.

For a long time he found himself staring thoughtfully at the door, but before he could frame a conclusion to his thoughts, Ribbon Peg entered, bearing a mop, a broom, and a pail.

"Miss Webster says I am to turn out your room and give it a good cleaning and then to change your sheets," she announced. "Ben's down in the kitchen heating water for you to

have a bath, soldier. *I* don't think you need
one, but Miss Webster says you do, so you'd
best go and have it."

She shifted from one foot to the other for a
moment and then blurted out, "Miss Webster's
a lady, ain't she?" in such wistful tones that
George, drawing on a borrowed dressing gown
several sizes too large, was forced to smile.

"She is that," he agreed.

An hour later, scrubbed and soaked, he was
sitting beneath the shade of an apple tree in
the yard by the pump, shaving himself in the
reflection of a mirror propped up on a chair,
when Miss Webster emerged from the house
accompanied by Princess Charlotte, who looked
considerably more cheerful than she had when
George had last seen her.

"Here, let me do that before you cut your
face to shreds," Elizabeth commanded, retriev-
ing Ben's razor from George's hand. He was
about to protest that he was perfectly capable
of shaving himself, but demurred from doing
so as Elizabeth gently pulled his head back
toward herself and expertly began to strop the
none-too-sharp razor as Charlotte seated herself on the well opposite him.

"I'm to say that I'm very sorry for having
spoken so rudely to you," the princess began a
trifle stiffly. "If you'll apologize for being so
high-handed with me!"

"George?" Elizabeth said.

"I'm sorry," George muttered warily.

Having accomplished this, the princess picked up a windfall apple from the grass and rubbed it against her skirt before biting into it with a hearty appetite. "Miss Webster explained to me that gentlemen don't like to be teased about such things as cutting a dash as a highwayman or going on the stage to play breeches parts," she continued ingenuously. "And I am very grateful to you for rescuing me from the Bristol Mail and looking after me, Lord Ventor."

"Major," Miss Webster reminded her with a look toward the house, where Blue had emerged from the kitchen door to toss out a pail of filthy water.

"Major," the princess repeated, tossing her head. "Miss Webster agrees that we must keep incognito as long as we are here."

"Miss Webster is quite right," George agreed.

"Miss Webster also says that I must let my father know where I am and that I am safe, so I will write a letter to his secretary, and she will see that it is posted."

"Very good," George said, submitting to Miss Webster's long, careful strokes with a sigh of comfort.

"And," the princess added, "I think Miss Webster's a great go, and far more up to snuff than that Ramplesham creature, which she did not tell me to say, but it is what I think!"

"Ma'am!" Elizabeth reproved her gently. It

was fortunate that George did not see the way in which her cheeks flamed scarlet.

"So," the princess continued angelically, "I have agreed to allow Miss Webster to guide my conduct and not tease you any further, because she don't preach and rail at one, or disapprove of the least little thing one wants to do. In fact, Miss Webster says that she thinks that I ought to be allowed more freedom than I have had, and if she were me, she would have done just what I did!"

George opened one eye to look at Miss Webster, but she firmly held his head in place by gripping one ear. "Do you want me to cut you?" she asked.

"I think you already have, Lizzie!"

"Nonsense," Elizabeth replied firmly.

From inside the Blood and Feather there was a great din and bustle, and Ben Stick emerged in his shirtsleeves, a look of disgust on his face as he crossed the yard toward the group beneath the tree.

"Well, Miss Webster, I don't know what you said or did, but you've got Ma all stirred up into a great bustle. She's *cleaning house*," he breathed in tones of great awe. "I've known Ma these past five years and more, and I've never seen her clean anything before!"

"You must admit, Mr. Stick," Elizabeth said mildly, "that a thorough cleaning certainly would not *hurt*."

Ben shook his long face. "She's got Red-Eye Jack and Blue scrubbing down the floors, and she and Peg are heating water to wash the linen! I don't know what the world's coming to! Before you know it, a nice quiet ken like the Blood and Feather will be *respectable*!"

His tone was so indignant that George was moved to laugh.

"Snarfle you might, soldier, but nothing will do for Ma but that I must goes and get some whitewash! Stagger me, but iffen I were to seek honest employment, it would not be as a housepainter!"

"Indeed, I should hope not!" Charlotte exclaimed sympathetically. "You should be a groom, at the very least!"

Ben looked appalled at the idea of honest toil, and walked off toward the stables, shaking his head and muttering to himself.

"Lizzie, whatever did you—?" George began to ask, but Miss Webster pressed a towel against his face, and his question was never answered.

10

Had he not passed a week beneath its roof, George would have been hard pressed to recognize the Blood and Feather for itself in the next few days. Under the mysterious influence of Miss Webster, the old inn had taken on a new character. Pine floors, concealed for years beneath layers of grime, suddenly shone, and diamond-paned windows, freshly washed, allowed the sunshine to penetrate into corners that had long sat neglected in darkness. The colors of rag rugs were beaten up again from years of dust, and curtains and sheets were boiled in the wash kettle and hung to dry, faded and worn but freed of mildew and dirt.

"Paying customers, soldier!" Ma Grimling exclaimed to Lord Ventor as he descended the stairs carefully one evening in order to dine in the private parlor with the princess and Miss

Webster. She jerked her head toward the common room, where a pair of fashionable-looking gentlemen lounged before the fire. "I had to send Blue over the hill to the farmer to get us a chicken and a ham, so we'll eat tonight!" she crowed. "The Blood and Feather will be respectable yet!"

"I must say you look quite respectable, Ma," George said, looking at her freshly starched mobcap an white muslin apron.

"It's *Mrs.* Grimling now, soldier," she replied. "No more Ma!"

George bowed. "Just as you wish," he said.

Mrs. Grimling nodded. "The ladies are in the parlor, and Peg'll be in with your dinner in a trice!" Importantly she bustled off to the kitchen, her chatelaine jingling at her waist.

The princess and Miss Webster were already ensconced in the private parlor, where a low fire burned in the newly cleaned grate and the furniture gleamed with lemon oil and spirit.

"It's *Mrs.* Grimling now," George repeated as he closed the door behind himself. "No more Ma! There are paying customers in the common."

"So we have heard," Charlotte replied, blue eyes dancing. "The Grimlings are determined to become respectable innkeepers! Do you see the pile of sheets Elizabeth and I have darned all day!"

Miss Webster looked up from the needlework in her lap. "Well," she said mildly, "we must do something to earn our keep, you know. Our funds are running very low."

George frowned at the idea of the princess and Elizabeth doing needlework, but Charlotte giggled. "I have always been the worst needle-woman in the world, so I'm afraid they have the bad end of the bargain," she admitted.

"Miss Prince would have preferred to muck out stables until I pointed out to her that that was out of the question," Elizabeth said.

"At least you don't want to run the high-ways with Ben anymore!" George said thank-fully, sinking into a chair and thinking what a cozy domestic picture they all made.

"Oh, I would, above all things, but Elizabeth would not like it," Charlotte replied, looking at her idol with adoration in her eyes.

"Nonetheless, I do not particularly like the idea that I cannot support us," George said. "Perhaps we ought to think on—"

At that moment Peg appeared in the room bearing a tray of sliced chicken and ham pies. Her toilette had also undergone a change for the better, in that she wore a neat dress of sprigged cambric with a modest décolleté and a flounce about the hem. As she laid the table, George was pleased to note that her hands were a great deal cleaner than they had been when last he saw her, and she smelled of soap and water rather than old linen.

"You should see the nobs in the common," she breathed excitedly. "All tuckered out in the first stare of fashion, they are, proper London gentlemen. An' they told me I was *pretty!*" She flushed with pleasure and retreated from the room.

"And so she is, when she bothers with herself," Miss Webster said, opening her napkin on her lap.

"Elizabeth scrubbed and scrubbed and I did her hair," Charlotte confided, setting to her food with a healthy appetite.

"And I suppose you attended to Blue's spots also?"

Elizabeth poured wine into clean, if chipped cuplets. "Mulrain and green soap," she said. "It never fails."

George helped himself to the ham. "I never knew you were such a complete hand, Lizzie," he said, looking at her across the table.

Her eyes rose to meet his for a second and then dropped to her plate, her expression unreadable. "Well, with no lady at the hall, a great many things fall to the rector's daughter, and one learns, you know, how things are supposed to be done. Besides, I have always held household for my father, ever since Mama died."

"Very true," George answered.

"Well, I know absolutely nothing about holding household," the princess admitted cheerfully. "I do know how to receive ambassadors, but that is perfectly useless in our present situation. I'll wager Lady Serena Ramplesham doesn't know how to get spots off."

"Ma'am," Elizabeth reproved gently, and Charlotte shrugged. "Well, I'll wager she doesn't know how to do anything except flirt and throw tantrums and shop," she said stubbornly.

"Very likely not," George sighed, "but if it were not for you, doubtless she would not have been so put out."

"Just you wait," Charlotte promised darkly. "She'll find out."

"I very much hope that she does not!" Elizabeth put in. "Only think what a scandal it would cause!"

"I never knew Mrs. Grimling was such a cook, after a week of watery stews and burnt breads," George said, savoring a haricot.

"It's *Mr.* Grimling who cooks. Evidently when he was a second-story man, he would take employment as a chef to case a house he intended to rob," Charlotte explained.

"Dear me," Miss Webster said, shaking her head. "I really must send him my compliments!" A hint of laughter danced about her face and George grinned at her, shaking his head.

"Dearest Lizzie," he said impulsively, gripping her hand. "You are the most complete hand

and the best friend anyone would ever hope for! What would I do without you?"

The smile suddenly dropped from her face, and she shook her head, withdrawing her hand from his. "Yes, I daresay I am a complete hand and the best of friends," she murmured. "Excuse me, please . . . the fire . . . so hot!"

She rose and exited from the room before George could protest.

The princess, who had been watching this exchange with interest, cast down her napkin and rose also. "I shall go to her," she said, turning at the door to look at the nonplussed George. "Why," she asked, "must men be such . . . such *men*?"

With that cryptic utterance, she hurled herself into the passageway after Elizabeth, barely avoiding a collision with a dandyish gentleman coming from the common room.

Clearly he was more than a little drunk, for he staggered backward against the wall, gaping up at Charlotte as she ran up the stairs.

"I say," he exclaimed loudly to George, who still was half out of his chair in the parlor, "if I didn't know better, I'd say that was the Princess of Wales! Know her anywhere. Well, not anywhere, actually"—he hiccuped—"but I do know her! Female could be her double!"

George felt a prickling along the back of his neck. He forced himself to smile casually. "Oh, everyone says there's a resemblance there," he said breezily.

The drunken dandy regained his balance with difficulty, preening his fobs and seals. "Daresay," he muttered, tiping a nonexistent hat toward George as he staggered down the hall toward the necessary.

George sighed as he lowered himself back into his chair, closing his eyes. It had been a narrow call.

How narrow, he had yet to discover, but feeling that he had handled the matter with dispatch and quick thinking, he settled down and put his feet against the grate, brooding upon the unpredictability of females and wondering what bug had suddenly taken hold of Elizabeth, who was not, in his experience, given to fits and starts.

Doubtless it had a great deal to do with the situation into which he had dragged her, he decided, downing his wine and refilling the glass. It certainly could not be easy on her. Only look at the way in which that other female, Lady Serena Ramplesham, had acted.

Indeed, he brooded, he had best begin to count himself fortunate that he had seen Lady Serena's true colors before he proposed to her. Indeed, it was impossible to picture Lady Serena Ramplesham as much as contemplating a visit to the Blood and Feather, let alone coming in and taking command of a damned impossible situation as Elizabeth had done. Lady Serena would have turned up her nose and called the constables, before collapsing in a tantrum or, at the very least, a strong fit of hysterics. In fact, it was very hard for George to contemplate Lady Serena Ramplesham doing anything more useful than ornamenting a drawing room full of her admirers. In fact, the more he reflected upon it, the more he began to realize that what he had considered sweetly childlike behavior in a beautiful woman was no more than the spoiled pets and vain conceits of an extremely selfish female. Unhappily he began to recollect how, when he had first begun to pay his addresses to her, she had received them with a marked indifference as long as the duke and the earl were dangling after her. Well, the duke had offered for an Irish heiress and the earl had cooled his ardor considerably after some time spent with Lord Ramplesham, and it was only then that Lady Serena had warmed to George, a mere viscount. And all the while, Lizzie had been there right beneath his nose, his best friend forever. What an irony it was that it had taken a misadventure such as this to make him realize what a wonderful female Lizzie was and always had been. Could it be that he was falling in love with her?

Before he had a chance to pursue this interesting line of thought any further, there was a knock at the door and Ben Stick thrust his head through the opening.

"Listen, soldier, I don't know what your game is," he said breathlessly, "but it's like as not that those two swells have tipped the dabs on you!"

George, startled out of his reverie, looked up. "What do you mean?" he asked.

For reply, Ben slipped into the room and thrust a newspaper beneath George's nose. "If this Miss Prince ain't as like as chalk to cheese to the royal princess, then I'm a snabbled gaffer!" he said firmly, and stood above George with his arms crossed over his thin chest as George perused the news sheet.

It was a *Morning Post*, and three days old, but when Lord Ventor spotted the engraving of Princess Charlotte on the page, his heart began to beat faster.

Nonetheless, he kept his voice calm as he handed the paper back to Ben. "I don't see what's so interesting about an old newspaper," he said casually.

Ben's basset-hound eyes turned down at the edges. "Then you're a bigger fool than I take you for, soldier, and I don't take you for much of a fool at all! One of them toffs had a look at your Miss Prince and immediately went off on everyone about how much she looks like Princess Charlotte—and so she does!"

"There is a resemblance," George admitted,

"but her mother, you know, was a grand friend of Prinny's."

Ben shook his head doggedly. "Her ma's no friend to the Prince, and well you know it, soldier. Everyone knows Princess Caroline don't fadge with Prinny!"

"If you'll look at the Court Circular, you'll see the Princess is on board one of the royal yachts at Weymouth, on holiday," George replied, trying to keep the tone of his voice bored.

Ben's long thin hands opened and closed. "Lookit, soldier, I'm not quite certain what your lay might be, but I do know that iffen you was to want to harm Miss, you've had chance and more to do it. If that chit's the daughter of a rich cit, then I'm King Midas . . . and I ain't!" He shook his head. "She's sommat more'n that, and there's no sense in tryin' to tell me she ain't!"

"Good God," Lord Ventor said, pushing a hand through his dark hair. "Who else has come to this conclusion?"

"No one yet, but it's only a matter of time. Think on, the Grimlings might talk about wantin' to be respectable, but scratch the surface and you'll find it's no good thing to throw temptation in their way—or mine! Why, you're no more eloping with Miss than I am!"

"The Grimlings," George repeated thoughtfully, stroking his chin.

"Aye, an' not just the Grimlings, but anyone

else who might come wandering through the door, soldier. There's those from London who like to come down here and hide away until the wind shifts in another direction, if you get my meaning."

"And a ransom—or worse—can go a long way to overcoming scruples."

"That's right, soldier. Now, I don't know what your lay is, and what's more, I don't want to know, because the less I know, the less there is to tell, think on, but it's as plain as a pikestaff that Miss Webster's a lady, and not the sort to be dragged into any sort of havey-cavey dealings."

"Don't think of it!"

"I don't, and what's more, neither should you, soldier! But I do know this! If I were you, I'd have those two morts out of this house before the cat could scratch, and I'd go as quick and quiet as I could. There's no sense in thinking that the leopard will change its spots, and Ma Grimling's a knowing one, think on!"

"I daresay you are right, Ben," George muttered thoughtfully, meeting the other man's eyes.

"I know I'm right! No sense in sayin' otherwise. It's all of a piece to me, you understand, but you do go get the ladies packed and together, and I'll sneck out and harness up your team, while the Grimlings is all drinkin' Hollands for supper."

"Thank you, Ben!" George said, gripping Ben Stick's hand in his own.

Ben Stick blinked, looking away. "Well, I'm right fond of Miss Prince—if that's what she chooses to call herself!—but I'll tell you this, soldier," he added wistfully. "If she weren't on the quality lay, she'd be a great one for the High Toby, and no mistake!"

11

"Narrow escapes in the middle of the night!" the princess said gleefully, huddled against the cold beside Elizabeth, who extended a protective arm about her shoulders as the phaeton, the three of them crowded into the narrow seat, bowled swiftly down the road, the sound of the horses' shod hooves the only sound in the chill and dark night.

"Narrow escapes!" Lord Ventor said between his teeth, peering into the narrow darkness of the road as he bent the leather about his fingers and rounded a corner on two wheels. "And thankful you should be for them, ma'am!"

"Oh, I am!" Charlotte promised rapturously, in no way daunted by the chilly evening. "After all, narrow escapes are a part of being royal, my lord! It is *always* so!"

"Perhaps in times long gone by, but cer-

tainly not in our day and age!" Elizabeth exclaimed. "We are civilized people, I should
hope, and not like some tinpot duchy in the
Balkans!"

"Oh, that is not at all what I meant," Charlotte corrected herself immediately. "But you
do not know what it is like, after spending a
lifetime cooped up and shackled to propriety
and governesses and protocol, to have—*finally!*—
adventures!"

"I begin to see," Elizabeth replied, barely
suppressing a smile. "Indeed," she added a bit
wistfully, putting a hand against the brim of
her bonnet to hold it to her head against the
wind, "I think it must be so for all females. I
know *I* have enjoyed having a bit of adventure."

George cast an odd look down at the top of
Miss Webster's bonnet, but said nothing. He
had never thought of Elizabeth as the sort of
female who would enjoy what she designated
an adventure.

"Well," said Princess Charlotte briskly, leaning toward Lord Ventor and Miss Webster with
all the air of a child being taken upon an excursion about the sights of London, "where are
we to next?"

Miss Webster and Lord Ventor exchanged a
look. George frowned thoughtfully. "Well, I
suppose the thing to do would be to wait until
your Mrs. Campbell returns to Bath, which I

hope will be soon, although I am of a mind to restore you to your worried parent at Brighton!"

"You would not do so!" the princess exclaimed indignantly. "That would be above all things odious!"

"Indeed, George," Miss Webster said calmly. "Since I have promised her royal highness that she may remain with me until she is restored to Mrs. Campbell, that would be unfair."

"What about my word? Do you know what grief this . . . this chit has caused me?" George exclaimed. "Hoyden!" he directed at the princess, who thrust out her tongue at him in a most unroyal gesture, which it was fortunate that he did not see. "I have been thrown out of the Rampleshams' house, wounded by a highwayman, and forced to depart from a hedge tavern in the middle of the night lest her true identity be discovered! Do you blame me for wishing myself well rid of her?"

"George! Lord Ventor! You are speaking about the future Queen of England!" Elizabeth said sternly, and Princess Charlotte grinned at him roguishly, just out of Elizabeth's line of vision.

"Well, then, you can keep her at the rectory until this Mrs. Campbell returns from the Lake District!"

Unruffled by George's gruffness, Miss Webster merely shook her head. "I should be glad to, but you know, even Papa might notice she was there, and I'm sure there would be questions that I should be hard pressed to provide answers for."

"Then what solution do you provide, Lizzie? For I tell you, *I* am at the end of my tether!"

Miss Webster laid a conciliatory hand upon George's arm. "Only be calm, and I shall lay out the plan I have conceived. Although I must admit it's very hard to think when one is roused up in the middle of ... well, one's dinner and told to pack everything and be ready to steal away within five minutes. I just keep looking over my shoulder, you know, half-expecting to see the Grimlings in hot pursuit!"

"Now, that would be famous!" the princess said.

"Indeed, it would not be at all famous, ma'am, and well you know it, so pray do not tease Lord Ventor any further!" Turning back to George, Elizabeth said, "I think the solution would be to keep her at Ventor."

"Keep her at Ventor? And you think there would be no questions about that?" George asked, incredulous.

"Far fewer than there would be at the rectory, certainly, George. For you know that everyone in the neighborhood is forever in and out of the rectory, not to mention all of Papa's sporting friends. Someone is bound to recognize her there. Whereas at the Hall, a gentleman living alone does not attract quite so many visitors, you know."

"Wonderful! I can see the look on Mrs. Fromish's face when I stroll in with a strange female on my arm! Lizzie, these people have been with my family forever! They aren't likely to look the other way—in fact, they are quite likely to get all sorts of ideas in their heads, and the next thing you know, the entire neighborhood will think that I'm . . . that I'm as bad as Trevor!"

"I doubt that anyone would ever see you as being quite *that* odious," Elizabeth said calmly. "But you will, of course, ask me to come stay at the manor, to bear, er, Miss Prince company. We shall say that your Aunt Augusta placed one of her nieces in your charge when you were in London, that you were to escort her back to her school in Bath. Alas, when you arrived in Bath, you found that this was not possible because . . . because . . ."

"There was an outbreak of smallpox!" Princess Charlotte interjected gleefully.

Elizabeth smiled at her. "An excellent suggestion . . . only perhaps something not quite so fatal—measles, perhaps?"

"Measles! That's the ticket!" George said. "By Jove, Lizzie, I never knew you had it in you to spin such banbury tales!" His tone was admiring.

"I would suspect there are a great many things you do not know about me," Miss Webster said softly, so softly that Lord Ventor did not hear her. "Anyway," she continued in a normal tone of voice, "I think it might be best if we were to remove that bandage from your head. You'll see that your graze is almost healed."

"We can tell everyone that he was kicked in the head by a horse," Princess Charlotte suggested.

"At least no one will suspect Charlotte is not a relation! Heaven only knows how many brothers and sisters your Aunt Augusta has, and I am certain that your people have never bothered to keep track of *all* of them," Elizabeth pointed out.

"I don't know why they should. *I've* never bothered to," George replied. "I don't even think Aunt Augusta knows precisely how many nieces and nephews she has." He gee'd up his team. "Well, at least I know where we're going, and glad it is I will be to see home again!"

12

When Lord Ventor awakened in the morning, it was not to the sound of Ben Stick's hoof-beats returning from a night on the High Toby, but to the sound of his own bed curtains being drawn back along the rail, exposing his face to a ray of warm sunshine rather than an inquisi-tive stare from Ribbon Peg, bearing lukewarm tea. For a moment he simply lay where he was, savoring the pleasure of his own down tick, his own bed, with his own clean sheets and freshly washed linen. When all was said and done, George was a man who enjoyed his home more than any other place on earth. Although years of soldiering had accustomed him to places far less comfortable, and even less clean than the Blood and Feather, he still felt that there was something to be said for—

"Good morning, my lord," said a funereal

145

voice, cutting sharply through his thoughts and placing him on warning.

Cautiously he opened one eye, to see Larousse, his valet, looking down his long pointed nose at his master, his wizened face set in an expression of forbidding correctness. Having known Larousse since boyhood, when the valet had served as second man of the chamber to his father, George also knew that forbidding correctness of manner well, and regarded him warily from beneath his lashes.

Mr. Larousse handed George a steaming cup of coffee from the tray beside the bed and watched as George sipped at the hot brown liquid. "Seeing as how you arrived home so late last night, and without any warning to myself or to Mr. Fishbank that there would be guests, it was decided to allow you to sleep in this morning," Larousse remarked, gazing at some point above the elaborately carved posts of the bed.

Certain now that he was in utter disgrace, George reached beneath the pillows and withdrew his watch. It lacked fifteen minutes to ten. "Good God!" he exclaimed, narrowly avoiding spilling coffee on those clean sheets as he swung his bare feet from the covers to the floor, where his slippers awaited him. "You must be angry with me, Larousse. Shall I also have to give my head for washing to Fishbank and Mrs. Gurney?"

"I do not understand what you mean, my lord," Mr. Larousse said, stropping George's razor in a rather precise sort of way, his back to his master. "We are all, after all, only servants in your house. It's not as if we haven't known you all your life, and Master Frederick and the old lord before you, after all," Larousse sniffed, and George knew he was in the soup.

"What has Miss Prince done? Where is Miss Lizzie? You don't need to pull those long faces on me, Larousse. I know when I'm in the soup."

Larousse held up George's dressing gown, a very plain affair of dark blue silk faced with claret, and allowed his master to slip into it before picking up his shaving mug, which he addressed with a vengeance. "I'm certain I don't know what you mean, sir," he said in arctic tones, pulling out George's chair for him and waiting until he had seated himself before pressing a hot towel against his stubble. "In fact, the general opinion belowstairs is that Miss Prince is a very taking lady, and of course, no one could be more welcome to those who have your best interests at heart than Miss Lizzie."

Buried beneath a towel, George muttered something, but before he could articulate, he was being briskly lathered, and his nose was grasped between an expert thumb and forefinger as Larousse dragged the razor along his jaw.

"Oh, it's not to say, sir, that anyone minds your leaving for London without so much as myself or even Naff accompanying you, although why you should want a groom to go to town with you is more than I could understand, and Naff so close to retirement ..." Briskly Larousse scraped about George's jaw and chin with deft, sure strokes. "But it is not at all what we expect in a gentleman's household, when not only is there no announcement in the *Post*, which Mrs. Gurney keeps by her very carefully, for she is very fond of the Court Circular, as you know, but when a lord of Ventor *disappears* without so much as a message for a fortnight, and then suddenly reappears with a strange young lady *and* a nasty head wound without so much as a by-your-leave—well, it is not at all what we expect, and we have been with the family, sir, since time out of hand!"

George's eyes rolled as he watched Larousse's progress, but he was unable to open his mouth to protest.

"Now, I must say, Master George," Larousse continued, "it's not my place to inquire into the doings of the lord of Ventor, nor is it anyone else's, either, but when you've been with a gentleman since he was in his cradle, and his father before him, as Mr. Fishbank, Mrs. Gurney, and I have, one realizes how gossip will travel, and some of the younger maids, not knowing any better, will say something to someone, and there you'll have it, sir." Larousse dabbed at George's face with an end of the towel, standing back to examine his handiwork. "Of course, Mr. Fishbank and Mrs. Gurney and I would never deign to gossip with the maids or stableboys. We belowstairs know what is due to our place, even if certain people do not!"

"Dear God!" George exclaimed with a mouthful of soap. "What dreadful act of lèse-majesté have I committed, that three of my oldest friends should be so out with me?"

Larousse, burying his master's face in another towel, sighed sadly. "Well, sir, Mrs. Gurney's cousin is by way of being cook at Lord Ramplesham's in Bath," he began, and was gratified to watch one of George's eyes fly open, glaring at him balefully. "Well, really, sir, speaking as one who has known you since your cradle, I think I might speak for all of those who have your best interests at heart when I say that *we*—that is, Mrs. Gurney, Mr. Fishbank, and myself—having known you—"

"I know how long you have known me, all of you!" George exclaimed, pulling the towel away from his face and looking up at the wizened face of his valet with something akin to impatience in his expression. "And I know how long you have been with my family, so out with it, Larousse! What's in the wind?"

Mr. Larousse swallowed several times, clearly torn between his position as a servant and his affection for his master. "Well, sir, I must say there are those of us who could never quite feel that Lady Serena would have been a proper Lady Ventor. You'll recall that when the Rampleshams visited here that Lady Serena and Lady Ramplesham went all about the house, without so much as a good word to say about anything, even things that have been in the family for generations, and spoke of putting decent folks who have spent their lives in Ventor service out to pasture—"

"Did she?" George asked dryly. "I did not notice."

"Well, of course you wouldn't, sir, bein' head over heels in love with Lady Serena at the time, and in spite of what hints those who have your best interests at heart tried to warn you away with," Larousse said impassively. "It is only that, well, it is not at all what we're used to in a gentleman's service, you see."

"You mean you have heard about that whole sordid episode! Good God, it must be all over the country by now!" George exclaimed.

Larousse used expert fingers to dab the lather away from George's cheeks. "Well, sir," he said, "it is only fortunate that you discovered, before it was too late, that Lady Serena is afflicted with moon madness."

"M-moon madness?" George repeated incredulously. "Lady Serena Ramplesham?"

"Indeed, sir, we understand what you have been through—how very distressing the entire sordid episode must have been for you, when your hopes were so high," Larousse said soothingly. "But only consider, sir, what the consequences might have been had you not discovered Lady Serena's, er . . . *fatal flaw* in time!"

Removing the towel from about George's neck, Larousse shook his graying locks. "Imagine mistaking a mere schoolroom miss like Miss Prince for the Princess of Wales! Indeed, sir, it is too much to ponder!"

"Too much indeed," George repeated in a shaking voice. "And you had all of this from Mrs. Gurney's cousin?"

"Oh, no, sir," Mr. Larousse said, setting his brushes to either side of George's head with expert strokes. "From Miss Prince herself. She thought it was quite a little joke, sir. As do we all who have your best interests at heart. If I may say so, however, the presence of ladies, particularly Miss Lizzie, at Ventor Hall is a welcome sign. May we expect to see some happy change in the near future?"

"Happy change?" George repeated suspiciously. "Is another of Miss Prince's thoughts that there will be a happy change?"

Larousse pressed his lips together. "That, sir, is not my place to say," he said firmly. "Shall we be dressing for dinner tonight?"

13

Oblivious of the interesting scene being enacted in Lord Ventor's chambers, Princess Charlotte and Miss Webster, having arisen early and breakfasted well upon eggs, kidneys, toast, and chocolate, were engaged in a vivacious game of battledore and shuttlecock on the south lawn.

Nothing could have presented a more charming picture than these two young females, their complexions shielded from the injurious rays of the autumn sun by leghorn hats (from Miss Webster's wardrobe), their morning gowns of white muslin (again, Miss Webster's, the princess's portmanteau being sadly deficient) shimmering prettily as they darted back and forth across the grass, pursuing the feathered shuttlecock across the court, laughing and calling to one another.

"Here he comes," the princess informed her

companion as she lobbed the shuttlecock back at Miss Webster, "and he looks rather plaguey. I wonder what I've done to cast him into the boughs now?"

"Come now," Elizabeth replied serenely, leaning out toward her left to return the volley, "George is not *always* so hipped as you might think!"

Unfortunately, at that moment George was waylaid by the ancient and garrulous gardener with a long list of questions or complaints concerning the orangery, a glass-and-brick monstrosity installed, like so much of the landscaping of the Hall, after the third viscount's Grand Tour. The sole function of the orangery, it would seem, was to consume enormous amounts of coke and wood, in return for which its trees infrequently, and only with great coaxing, produced small inedible bits of fruit.

He was so long about this that the princess and Miss Webster were able to conclude several games, in which the princess trounced her opponent roundly more often than not, and losing interest, strolled along the herbaceous-bordered paths, beneath the brilliant chestnut trees in full golden foliage, toward the ornamental lake, another of the third viscount's innovations.

It was here that George finally caught up with them, about to embark on the black and somewhat clogged waters in a small rowboat provided for that purpose.

"Good morning," Elizabeth said with a smile as George approached them. "You are just in time to row out to the island with us!"

"Punting would be more like it," George said ruefully, looking at the weeds which choked the bottom of the water. "Good morning! I trust I find you both well?"

"Indeed," the princess replied demurely as George assisted her to board the rowboat. "No ghostly presences, no sinister servants rendered my night hideous. And alas, Lord Ventor, no highwaymen." She settled herself on the little seat, pulling her skirts away to clear a place for Miss Webster, who followed her.

George climbed aboard after them, using the oar to push the boat away from the shore. "Now," he said carefully, "I must inform you that my man told me this morning that you were going about telling the servants that Lady Serena Ramplesham was mad!" Fitting the oars into the locks, he glowered at the princess, who gave him a most regal stare, her eyes as blue as the sky.

"I said nothing at all to your *man*," she drawled lazily, trailing a hand through the water, "but I did happen to remark to Mrs. Gurney, your housekeeper and a most amiable woman, I might add, that any female who would mistake a mere Miss Prince for the Princess of Wales was obviously not in her right mind. Considering that she had had a letter from her cousin, who is employed by the Rampleshams, detailing our evening there in rather lurid terms, I thought it was the *least* I could do."

"You did not!" Miss Webster gurgled, putting up her parasol to hide a suspiciously improper expression. "You wretched girl, whatever did you mean?"

"Well, if you were to ask me, Lady Serena Ramplesham *is* out of whatever mind she has. The female is utterly moonstruck, and a faint-heart into the bargain," Charlotte said contemptuously, raising one eyebrow in a Hanoverian manner. "Obviously, I am Miss Prince, and *hardly* the Princess of Wales, whom all the world knows to be in Weymouth at this very moment!" Her point made, she flicked up her own parasol. "Besides, any female who would cast aside Lord Ventor is obviously a moonling."

George, who had been about to launch into a tirade, was forced to see the wisdom of the princess's position. Doubtless such a ripe and juicy story was all over Bath, and scandal-broth could only be mitigated by ruthlessly casting Lady Serena's character to the winds. As he came to think about it, Lady Serena had *not* behaved very well at all! His eyes fell upon Elizabeth, and somewhat to his own amazement, he heard himself saying, "Indeed, ma'am, I think you are right. Lady Serena Ramplesham never would have done for me at all."

Elizabeth's eyes met his, but George could

not hold her gaze, for he suddenly felt something deep and regretful inside himself that he could not properly examine, save that he felt that it was too late to even hope in that direction.

"Shall we go out to the ornamental island?" the princess, oblivious, inquired.

With some effort, George tore his attention away from Elizabeth and concentrated upon the princess. "As with most of Ventor, it is in a shocking state of disrepair, as you may see. There was an ornamental hermit who lived on the island in my father's day, but when we were small, he died, and I doubt that even the most wretched vagabond would care to replace him, for the hermitage is occupied now by rats and squirrels, and quite overgrown."

"An ornamental hermit! What an Augustan notion!" the princess exclaimed, laughing.

"I think you will find a great deal at Ventor that is positively Georgian," Elizabeth said, and George threw her a sharp look, but she seemed oblivious of him, lightly taking up the threads of history where he had left them off, as if she had been born at the Hall. She may as well have been, George realized, for she knew every inch of it, from the long habit of easy intercourse that had always existed between the rectory and the estate. As she was discoursing on the adventures of the Mad Viscount, who was reputed to have ridden up from London, smothered his wife with a pillow, and ridden away again, it was forcibly borne in upon George that Miss Webster knew his estates as well as or better than he did himself. It was easy to see her as mistress of Ventor Hall . . . indeed, suddenly far easier to see Elizabeth installed here than Lady Serena Ramplesham, who had never really seemed to *fit* into life at the Ventor Hall. George could just imagine the consternation among the servants if *she* had appeared with a strange female in tow. But if *Miss Lizzie* did so, then surely it was all right!

From the very moment that Lizzie had appeared at the Blood and Feather to unpick the tangle into which he had wrapped himself, he had begun to realize his folly in selecting a spoiled and selfish beauty such as Lady Serena Ramplesham. That lady's conduct when he appeared with the princess in tow had done nothing to endear her further to him. Indeed, she had finally flown her true colors and exposed herself for what she truly was. Dearest Lizzie, on the other hand, had asked no questions, but had set out to make all right and proper. And it was only now that he began to realize that he was falling head over heels in love with his best friend.

Now was hardly the time to hope that Lizzie might reciprocate his feelings. What female likes to be proposed to when she knows that a

man has just been summarily rejected by another? Certainly Lizzie, who saw a great deal
with those placid green eyes, would instantly
reject his suit as a consequence of his rebound-
ing from Lady Serena, and that would not do!
Nor, he doubted, would she believe him when
he tried to explain that, had he any sense at
all, he would have offered for her in the first
place rather than coming home from the wars
and offering for a London belle whose only
concerns were fashion and appearance.

Well, perhaps he should wait until the princess had been placed back with her governess
in Bath. By his calculations, Mrs. Campbell
ought to be returning from the lake District in
a very few days. Once her highness, and her
royal fits and starts, had been placed into the
capable hands of Mrs. Campbell, then perhaps
things would return to normal and Lizzie might
be induced to listen to his proposal.

He was gazing at her fondly when Miss Webster suddenly cut herself off in the middle of a
discourse concerning the establishment of the
formal gardens to snap her parasol closed and
exclaim, "Good God, George, is that Trevor
standing at the foot of the lake and waving in
this direction?"

14

"I say, coz, when old Fishbank told me you was out here rowin' around, I didn't know what to think," Trevor Worthington drawled as George reluctantly rowed the small boat back toward the bank. " 'Servant, Lizzie, Miss ... uh, Miss ... ?"

"Miss Prince, my cousin Trevor Worthington," George sighed, tossing Trevor the mooring line. "With, I might add, his usual sense of bad timing."

The princess surveyed Trevor from head to heels, evidently liking what she saw very much, from his gleaming Hessians to his well-pomaded strawberry locks.

"Oh, I wouldn't say it was bad timing at all," Trevor said, looking at the princess and liking what he saw also, as he handed her out of the boat.

"What brings you into the country again so soon, Trevor? It will, of course, be a short visit?" Miss Webster said brightly, only her shrewd eyes conveying a hidden message.

As usual, Trevor was impervious to hints, especially from Miss Webster. Being possessed of a supreme conceit to match his good looks, he would not have believed her if she had informed him that he left her cold, but instead, had always assumed, and Trevor was a great one to assume, that when he was finished sowing his wild oats, Elizabeth and her considerable fortune would fall into his hands like ripened fruit. The slings and snubs that she hurled in his direction fell, as they always had, away from a toughened hide impervious to insult.

"Rusticating, you know," he explained to the company in general, with a light shrug of one well-tailored shoulder. "Thought m'cousin George would put me up for a week or so. His people told me that there was a female cousin here visiting, but I don't believe we've met, Miss Prince."

"She is a *fraternal* cousin," George said. "Waiting to join her governess in Bath."

Charlotte was staring at Trevor in a way that Miss Webster could not like, so with a flip of her parasol she put her hand into the princess's elbow. "I believe you have not seen the portrait galleries," she said. "We shall go and inspect them next."

Charlotte smiled at Trevor and Trevor smiled at Charlotte. "Shall we see you at lunch, Mr. Worthington?" she asked.

"Never miss a meal," Trevor promised, and with a long, evil look which he was able to attribute to jealousy, Miss Webster drew the princess firmly up the lawn, much to George's relief.

"All right, Trev, what's it all about?" George demanded flatly.

Trevor, lifting his quizzing glass for a last admiring look at the princess's retreating figure, sighed in appreciation and shook his head. "I heard in Bath that all the world was buzzing about you showing up with a female at Serena Ramplesham's," he said. "La Ramplesham's going about claiming it's the Princess of Wales, and the *on-dit* is that she's quite mad . . . but by God, George, that's no cousin to you!"

"Niece of my father's sister Augusta. Goes to school in Bath. And by heaven, Trev, if you try to start up one of your flirtations with a schoolroom miss, well, there won't be any accounting for what I'll do to you!"

"No, I daresay not!" Trevor agreed, and his grin told George he had no more believed his story than any other banbury tale. "However, it don't signify! Thing of it is, coz, that little high flier I chased to Bath cost me an arm and a leg and left me high and dry for a rich cit in the bargain! Seems as a punishment for my dereliction of duty at that reception for the *real* Princess of Wales, m'enraged parent is refusing to advance me as much as a groat until quarter day! So, old boy, I'm yours until then!"

"Oh, no you're not! I won't have you in the same house with Lizzie and a schoolroom chit, by God!"

"Come, George, old man, do be a sport," Trevor said jovially to his cousin. "I'm fairly certain you don't want to see your dearest coz hung up in debtors' prison, do you? I'm burnt to the socket, old man!" Trevor shook his head and gave his cousin his most charming smile. "Anyway, dear fellow, my last high flier cost me everything I own." He polished his nails on the lapel of his brown coat, the finest example of the art of Nugee, with padded shoulders and ridiculously full tails, his long lashes dropping over his eyes as he smiled slyly up at his massive cousin, who was looking none too pleased. "Anyway, old man, I swear to you, this is the last time I shall impose upon your good nature. I am seriously thinking that I must marry and settle down."

George was moved to a burst of laughter. "What? *You?*" he asked, none too credulous. "Don't bam me, Trev! This time you are doing it a bit too brown!"

Trevor shook his pomanded locks from side to

side, his smile beatific. "Oh, no! I promise you I'm not! Time and enough that I was settled down and married, George. Even you must admit that. Besides, it will get my mother off my back! You can't imagine how she's been taking on lately, telling me that I must marry!"

"I can't imagine the female alive that would have *you!*" George said baldly.

Mr. Worthington's ego was sufficiently bloated to enable him to laugh jovially, as if Lord Ventor had made a great jest. "Ah! You were always such a one, George, but it's true, I have decided that I must break the hearts of every female of my acquaintance and settle upon just one."

George puffed his cheeks in and out, torn between laughter and exasperation. "And who, may I ask," he said carefully, when he trusted himself to speak again, "is the lucky lady?"

"Why, Lizzie, of course!" Trevor said, as if his cousin were a very great fool indeed. "Who else? Only think upon it! Why, she is almost upon the shelf, she is possessed of no mean fortune, and she has been in love with me ever since we were very small!" So sublime was Trevor's confidence that it was all that George could do not to burst out laughing. For as long as he could recall, Lizzie had been vocal and firm in her dislike of his cousin. Indeed, her dislike of Trevor was only matched by his own.

"That is the most preposterous thing I have

ever heard!" George exclaimed. "Good God, Trev, you must be touched in the noggin if you think Lizzie would ever consent to marry you!"

"Well, why shouldn't she?" Trevor asked, in no way shaken by his cousin's reaction. "Only think upon it! I am possessed of superior birth and breeding. I do not wish to sound my own horn, but my looks are far more than merely passable, and my *ton* impeccable; I may be seen anywhere. I must admit that my finances are somewhat complicated at present, but since she will come into her mother's fortune upon marriage, that need not concern me overmuch, for she will enable us to live in the style to which I am accustomed. My address is charming, and certainly, since Lizzie is a woman of the world, she will not expect to see me at home every night of the week, nor enact me a Cheltenham tragedy if I continue to pursue what barques of frailty continue to cross my path. In short, I will offer the cachet of becoming Mrs. Trevor Worthington, and she will offer me her fortune. What could be more agreeable?"

George reached into his pocket and withdrew his pocketbook. From its leather interior he drew out several notes and pressed them into Trevor's hand. "Take this and leave! Go to London or Bath or Melton, I care not where you rest yourself, but simply remove yourself from Ventor at once!"

Trevor's eyebrow raised slightly and he

looked at the bills in his hand, counting them carefully before he replied. "Cutting it up stiff, coz!" he remarked airily. "I always knew you were jealous of me, but I never knew quite how much until this moment! Don't tell me you've set your cap at the fair Lizzie, not after that little scene you enacted with Serena in Bath! Doing it a bit, coz! And anyway, who is that bit of fluff you've got Lizzie here protecting for you? I know all your cousins on both sides, George, and *she* ain't one of them! Found yourself an heiress to paste this ramshackle place back together, perhaps?"

"Trevor," Lord Ventor said narrowly, "I will not have you in the same house with Lizzie, let alone Miss Prince, so be a good sort and take yourself off right now, or I damned well fear I shall have to plant you a solid facer!"

Trevor lifted an elegant shoulder, looking down at the money in his hand. "My, my, my, I do seem to have touched a nerve, do I not?" he asked lightly. "Don't tell me you and Lizzie are smelling of April and May, because, dear boy, I simply shan't believe it!"

George made a gesture as if to grasp the fine lapels of Trevor's jacket into his fist, and his cousin took a delicate step backward. "I say, no need for fisticuffs! That's the trouble with all of you! You go to Jackson's Boxing Salon, you Corinthians, and then you feel ready to ruin a perfectly good jacket, simply because a man speaks his mind to his cousin! Bit much, old boy! Much as I'd like to keep your filthy lucre, however, I'm run to ground at present! Nowhere else I can go! They've barred me from everywhere until quarter day, and frankly, old man, there are a number of places I'd rather not go, lest I run into some of the people to whom I owe a number of debts from New-market . . . I mean to say, you do see, old man, don't you? I've got no choice but to rusticate for a while."

"Trevor, this is not the time or the place! Turning you loose at Ventor Hall while two females are beneath my roof with only Mrs. Gurney as chaperone is like . . . well, dash it, it's just not done!"

Trevor folded his hands together prayerfully. "I shall be as good as the driven snow!" he promised. "The ladies shall be safe!"

"I will *not* have you bothering Lizzie, nor Miss Prince, either!" George insisted sternly.

"I shall be as a monk while I am beneath your roof," Trevor promised.

"See that you are, Trevor, because if you're not, I can promise you that I'll have your liver and your lights nailed to the barn door!"

"Dear me, coz, no need to be so violent! We are, after all, *family!* It is only for a few days, until things die down a little in certain quarters!"

"By God, Trevor! If the bailiffs come to Ventor again looking for you, I'll—"

"Oh, nothing quite that bad, I assure you, dear coz!" Trevor said soothingly. "Only the merest matter of having swallowed a spider until quarter day, I assure you! Run of bad luck at Newmarket! You see, there was a horse called Blood-and-Thunder and—"

"Don't tell me!" George implored wearily. "The less I know about your wastrel life, the better for both of us! But if you are going to stay *here*, Trevor, I warn you, the slightest hint of impropriety, and family or no, you're out! Forever and good, and don't think I'm jesting, because I am *not*, I promise you!"

"Oh, believe me, I shall be as milksopped and proper as you could wish! Not a word out of me shall you hear, old boy," Trevor promised breezily. "But just in case . . ." With nimble fingers he removed the bills he had pressed into George's hand and made them disappear into his own pocket so quickly that George blinked. "Perhaps, you know, when this is all blown over, I ought to pay my court to Serena Ramplesham! *She's* a fashionable girl who knows the ways of the world!"

"I wish you luck of the venture!" George said fervently. "You and Lady Serena deserve each other, if you ask me. But if I hear so much as a whisper from one of my people that you've been plaguing Lizzie or Miss Prince with

169

your unwelcome attentions, I'll lay you a facer that will plant you into next week! See if I don't!"

"Oh, no fear of that, cousin! No female under your roof shall receive any unwelcome attentions from Trevor Worthington, I can promise you that!"

George regarded his cousin narrowly, but Trevor's face was as innocent as it was possible for any Worthington to look. "I hope," George said, somewhat mollified, "that you've learned your lesson, Trev!"

"Oh, you may certainly believe me when I say that I have!" Trevor promised breezily. Beneath his breath, he added to George's stolidly retreating back, "And believe me, dear coz, I shall take care to teach you one also!"

Gratitude was not one of Trevor's virtues.

15

Although George had little time to watch him like a hawk over the next several days, he had to admit, upon the occasions when he found Trevor in company with Lizzie and the princess, that his cousin's behavior, for once, was unexceptionable. Since Miss Webster had also made up her mind to watch Trevor carefully, George was able to feel slightly more sanguine about his incognito charge.

Although the circumstances were somewhat unusual, the air of a house party very soon began to prevail, and Mrs. Gurney, shuffling about with her chatelaine at her waist, was heard to remark to Mr. Fishbank that it did her a world of good to see Master George entertaining young persons at Ventor again. That those three persons in his service who had his affairs at heart also kept a stern, if surreptitious eye upon Trevor Worthington might also have assisted in keeping him in line, for at no time in the next several days did he find himself alone with either Elizabeth or the princess without some servant suddenly discovering an errand in that vicinity.

If Trevor was aware of these protective devices thrown up against him, he made no comment, but rather exerted himself all the more to utilize his much-vaunted charm to the utmost, exercising it against all and sundry.

Thus, pleasant autumn days were passed without notable incident, which was precisely how Elizabeth and George would have wished it to be, their principal aim being to restore their royal charge to her governess undamaged in any way by her adventures, and certainly without any scandal or gossip attached to her name.

For her part, the princess seemed to enjoy herself immensely, joining Miss Webster for breakfast each day at nine, during which repast she daily put away such a healthy assortment of grilled kidneys, kippers, bacon and eggs, sausage, muffins, and black coffee laced with sugar that Miss Webster was moved to wonder where she kept it all. After breakfast the ladies would stroll the grounds and play battledore-and-shuttlecock, a sport that Miss Webster would have considered beneath the contempt of such a dandy as Trevor Worthington had he not taken to relieving her in playing the indefatigable princess and providing far better competition than she herself could muster. Mr. Worthington was also most anxious to row the ladies about the lake, a gesture Miss Webster was certain arose from utter boredom, although even she had to admit that Trevor could be utterly charming when he chose, and that his company went a great way to keep Miss Prince from the sort of boredom that inevitably led to her worst acts of mischief. Mrs. Gurney did her best to provide a nuncheon repast that would meet the healthy appetite of a growing girl, and again, Elizabeth opened her eyes very wide at the amount of cold beef, mutton, cheese, bread, and fruit pastries Charlotte could consume without causing ill effects upon her figure or energies, for in the afternoon they either rode horseback with the gentlemen or she accompanied Miss Prince as she expertly tooled George's phaeton about the estate, taking an avid interest in its management. It was coming closer and closer to harvest time, and George was anxious as to the state of his corn, the crop upon which the economy of Ventor depended. That he could wax entirely too voluble upon the subject of agriculture for the city-bred tastes of his cousin Trevor meant that this gentleman frequently retired for his afternoon nap, but always Trevor reappeared at dinner, resplendent in his evening dress and smooth as cream in his manners, so much so that he was able to keep them all feeling very witty throughout the meal, even cracking a smile from George from time to time. Here, the princess did full justice to whatever menu Mrs. Gurney had decided to put before her, and Mrs. Gurney, who appreciated a healthy appetite, as well as the judgment of a gourmet like Trevor, exerted herself to produce the very best meals that she could.

So long had Lord Ventor lived in bachelor solitude that she had had to content herself with a joint and only one or two removes, but now, with company in the house, her frustrated artistry burst forth, and the dinner table groaned beneath such delicacies as lobsters, venison roasts, dressed crab, duck in aspic, and such a variety of removes and courses that even the appetite of the princess was satiated.

Fishbank, muttering that it was quite like the old lord's days, raided the wine cellar for the finest stores to match the finest food, and succeeded so well that even Trevor was moved to send his compliments to both butler and housekeeper.

After dinner, Elizabeth played at the pianoforte, having all of the latest music at her command, including the new and daring waltz that had come from Vienna, and Trevor, with one eye on George's glowering face, delicately waltzed Miss Prince about the drawing room, teaching her the graceful, gliding steps. The princess, a workmanlike, if uninspired player, in turn spelled Elizabeth, so that Trevor might teach her also, and if George glowered all the more to see Miss Webster swirling between the furniture in the arms of his libertine cousin, she would then insist that George must learn to waltz.

Lord Ventor, treated to the sensation of at last holding Miss Webster, somewhat awkwardly, in his arms, looked down at her with an uneasy smile, feeling the blood flushing into his face.

"Do dance, Lord Ventor!" the princess commanded, pounding at the pianoforte with a great deal of enthusiasm, if not expertise; at least she kept the beat, and that was all that was required.

"I say, coz, you must oblige the lady!" Trevor added, seating himself professorially in a chair and plumping up his neckcloth.

"Come, George, or you shall be utterly out of step!" Elizabeth teased, and proceeded to guide him about the floor.

George's interests had always been military, and his manner was somewhat brusque for the drawing room, but with Elizabeth lightly guiding him, he surrendered to the dance, and very soon found himself given over to the rhythm of the thing.

"I say!" he exclaimed, rather pleased with himself.

"You are doing very well!" Elizabeth encouraged him, looking up at his broad, good-natured countenance with sparkling eyes, two bright pink spots of excited color in her cheeks.

"Only because *you* are here to teach me!" he exclaimed, and Elizabeth dropped her eyes, lest he read the look in their green depths.

On the nights when they did not dance, they spent the time playing whist for outrageous, imaginary stakes, and Trevor and the princess proved to be by far the shrewder players, perhaps because it ran in their blood.

Only when Mrs. Gurney sent in the tea tray at eleven-thirty did the party break up, Miss Webster carefully chaperoning the princess up the stairs to bed, George and Trevor drowsing indifferently over their brandy until, at last, they too retired.

Whatever was in the back of Trevor's mind seemed to stay there, for nothing could have been more civil than his outward conduct. But Trevor was Trevor, and he was biding his time, waiting for his moment. For several days he had been watching the other members of the houseparty, in particular George and Elizabeth. In some way intrinsic to his nature he understood how the wind stood in that corner, and felt not only a vague sense of foreboding but also an outright sense of ill-use that Miss Webster, who should, by his own calculations, have been his now that he had finally decided the time had come for him to settle down and marry a respectable female, instead seemed to prefer his decidedly less handsome, less fashionable, and distinctly uncharming cousin George. In Trevor's mind, what Trevor desired, Trevor should have, and morality and propriety had nothing at all to do with the matter. From birth he had been pampered and cosseted by parents who had long since despaired of producing anything but daughters, and nothing in the course of his life had led him to believe anything could stand between himself and those things which he sought to possess as his own. Therefore, since Miss Webster made it obvious that she reciprocated Lord Ventor's feelings, it seemed to Trevor that he needed to avenge this deliberate slight to his person.

Like the spoiled child that he essentially was, Trevor had begun to cast about for some method of revenge, and not unnaturally, he settled upon Miss Prince as the most likely target.

Not for a moment did Trevor believe that Miss Prince was merely a cousin of George's; as he had informed Lord Ventor, he knew his own and George's relations far too well for that. Nor did he believe Miss Prince was Miss Prince, in spite of every effort made to convince him to the contrary. Indeed, worldly-wise Trevor had very quickly formulated the opinion that Miss Prince's manners were hardly those of a schoolroom chit. Know it or not, he decided George and Elizabeth had been bammed by some sort of adventuress, for he mistook, in his own arrogance, the manners of a princess of the house of Hanover for those of a very fast sort of girl, precisely the sort of female who would easily succumb to his well-practiced blandishments.

Without stopping to think, for thought had never been Trevor's long suit, a plan began to form in his head that was, by his lights, *not really so very bad*, as he told himself, and in fact, really doing old George a whopping great favor, if you looked at it the right way. Why, George positively ought to be *thanking* him!

The princess herself unwittingly contributed to Trevor's mischief, when upon rising quite early one morning, and finding herself alone at the breakfast table, she sent word to the stables to harness up George's phaeton and team, an unexceptionable command, since it was well known that George admired her driving skills.

Upon returning upstairs to change into her habit, and descending the stairs again, nattily attired in bottle-green broadcloth, with frogs and epaulets *à la militaire* in gold braid, and her hair tucked up beneath a toque, Charlotte presented a pretty figure when she encountered Trevor in the hallway, still yawning as he sought his morning coffee.

"Well, hello, what have we here?" he asked, surveying the princess appreciatively from head to toe through his quizzing glass. "Out for a ride, hey?"

Charlotte, not impervious to Trevor's good looks and charm, and completely innocent as to the true nature of his character, smiled encouragingly. "I was of a mind this morning to take out the phaeton for a little ride. It is such a nice day that I thought one might enjoy the countryside."

Trevor's eyes narrowed for a second, and a second only, before he offered his arm, impeccably clothed in sky-blue bath superfine, to the princess. "A morning such as this should not be enjoyed without company! You will permit me to join you?"

Heedless, Charlotte nodded her assent, and in a very short time George's phaeton bowled down the driveway at a spanking pace.

Nothing could have been more proper than Trevor's conduct during their ride over the narrow roads and byways surrounding Ventor Hall. He limited his speech to the most commonplace remarks and chance civilities, and in no way exercised his well-known charms or powers of seduction. That, he decided, would come later; time enough now to simply lay the foundations for his plans. He was attentive to all that Miss Prince said, and highly complimentary of her skill with the team, although he himself was an indifferent whipster, and in every way presented himself as the picture of jovial, nonthreatening companion.

For her part, the princess was almost subdued, casting many thoughtful looks at her companion, and gracefully deflecting any delicate questions about herself by countering with a question about Trevor, and since he was his own favorite subject, he was only too happy to respond, and at length, concerning himself, his impeccable *ton*, and his fashionable friends, perhaps in the belief that Charlotte would find this résumé impressive.

They drove through Hand Cross and over toward St.Mary's without incident, and returned the same way they had come, when the sun was placed about noon in the sky.

Entering the house by a side door, they were greeted by the funereal countenance of Fishbank. "Ah, miss, there you are!" he said. "I'm sure that Miss Lizzie and milord will be glad to know that you have returned without incident! They are waiting for you in the morning room, if you please." Fishbank swallowed before adding, "Not you, Mr. Trevor."

Thinking, not unnaturally, that some word had come from her governess, Miss Prince slung the tail of her habit over her arm and bustled down the hallway toward that chamber.

Mr. Worthington, left behind without so much as a by-your-leave, thrust his hands into his pockets and whistled tunelessly.

"Good morning!" the princess announced as she entered the morning room, where Lord Ventor was seated at the table, looking thunderous, and Miss Webster halted in the act of pacing the room to look at her with such a lugubrious expression that she at once suspected some terrible disaster had befallen her family.

"Is . . . is it Papa? Or Gran'mama?" she stammered, a great deal taken aback.

"Nothing so bad as that—" Elizabeth began to say, but Lord Ventor, looking every bit as Romanish as the Regent himself, slowly rose to his feet and cleared his throat, his countenance turning a port-wine red.

"How could you behave so?" he asked. "Do you but stop and consider making of yourself a spectacle for every gape-box and prattlemonger between here and Ottery St. Mary's? Good God, ma'am, think of yourself, if not of Miss Webster and me."

Elizabeth moved quickly forward, laying a hand upon the princess's shoulder. "George is quite put out with you for taking his phaeton without his permission, my dear—we have been quite ill with worry."

"Not only to take the phaeton, but to take up that rakehell cousin of mine," George sputtered, exasperated. "And just when I thought you were beginning to display some common sense!"

Charlotte, not unnaturally, began to feel very much put upon by this unexpected attack. In all innocence, she had no idea that she had committed any sin whatsoever; now to find herself offered recriminations for what seemed to be a perfectly innocent action made all her hackles stand upon end, and eighteen years of royal upbringing rushed into the gap.

"You must forgive me," she drawled, pulling off her gloves, "for I certainly meant to give no offense, only employed what I had been given to understand was my privilege to use. If Mr. Worthington chose to accompany me, it would hardly be civil to refuse him. Indeed, Lord Ventor, he provided me with a most proper escort!" She stood at her full height, her blue eyes flashing fire at George, every inch the princess.

Elizabeth, somewhat put out at both the princess and Lord Ventor, automatically sought to mediate. "It is for your own good that Lord Ventor is worried, you know. Suppose that you were to meet with an accident, or be recognized by someone—"

"Me? An accident?" the princess exclaimed. "I'm a fine whip! Ask anyone!"

At the same time, George said, "It's not that I don't trust you, ma'am—capital sort of horsewoman and all of that! It's my cousin you can't trust! Devil of a fella!"

If her nose had not been put so severely out of joint, the princess, who had, in general, every reason to respect Lord Ventor's judgment, might have been constrained to listen to reason. Her own instincts about people, which were very good, had warned her that Trevor Worthington was something of a loose fish. However, when confronted in such a high-handed way by George, with her trusted Elizabeth seeming to back him up, for crimes she did not consider that she had committed, she could only see red.

Speech failed her; with a haughty toss of her head she turned and walked majestically out of the room, feeling that Mary, Queen of Scots, on her way to the headsman could not have done any better.

George was left to watch as the door closed behind her, the muscles in his jaw working tightly.

"Perhaps I ought to go to her," Elizabeth suggested.

"Yes! Perhaps you ought ... No, wait!" George replied, seizing Elizabeth by the wrist. "For the past fortnight, you and I have played

183

governess to that chit, Lizzie, and I, for one, find the chore wearing me down. I had meant to wait until Mrs. Campbell had reclaimed her, but this will wait no longer! Lizzie, will you stroll in the gardens with me?"

Miss Webster looked up at George's face, read his pleading expression, and temporarily abandoned her mission. The princess, she knew from experience, would retire to her bedchamber to indulge in a fit of sulks, and would, if tempted with some new treat, such as the sight of goldfish in the ornamental lake or an excursion to see the Roman ruins, emerge in a sunny humor, ready to forgive and be forgiven by George, whose own naturally sanguine temperament would soon reassert itself also.

She had not the faintest idea why George wanted her to walk in the gardens with him; she supposed that he wanted her assistance in devising some tactful plan that would rid Ventor Hall of the detested Trevor; so, in her old plain white muslin round gown and a rather shabby shawl that had seen much use, she dutifully allowed him to escort her through the French doors into the glories of the outdoors.

It was a grand and beautiful day. A crisp morning frost had given way to a sunshine bright and warm enough for summer, and as they walked down the gravel path from the terrace to the lake, George offered Elizabeth his arm.

She slipped her hand into the crook of his elbow and lifted the ruffled hem of her skirt slightly above the path. "The Michaelmass daisies are lovely this year," she remarked in her serene voice.

"I particularly like the asters and the dahlias. M'mother put in those borders, you know," George said thoughtfully.

"I don't think that there is day that goes past that I do not miss your parents," Elizabeth replied. "They were like an aunt and an uncle to me. Ventor is as dear to me as if it were my own house."

"I wish it were your own house!" George said suddenly and awkwardly, blushing from his neck to his hairline.

Elizabeth was suddenly self-conscious about her old muslin and even older shawl. Her eyes dropped to the gravel beneath her feet, and she studied the toes of her slippers as they slowly paced past the holly borders. She knew not what to think at all, and her face drained of color.

"I know this must seem strange—not at all in the habit of the petticoat line! Well, I ain't Trevor!" George said desperately.

"Thank goodness for that," Elizabeth said simply.

"You really think so?" George looked at her, much encouraged. "I mean, you don't have a *tendre* for Trevor or anything like that, do you?"

Elizabeth was so astonished that she stopped and looked at him, her green eyes very wide. "What? A *tendre* for Trevor?" she asked, thoroughly incredulous, and then burst into laughter. "I am excessively sorry," she managed to say between bursts of laughter, "for I know that he is your cousin, but *nothing* would induce me to develop a *tendre* for Trevor!"

"I see," George said, much relieved. In a brighter, more hopeful tone, he added, "You are not inclined toward anyone else, are you?"

"There was a man," Miss Webster sighed, putting up her parasol, "but he was promised to another."

Mentally George reviewed all of the gentlemen of Elizabeth's acquaintance. "Was it Snowhill?" he asked.

The corners of Miss Webster's lips trembled. "Snowhill was three years older than Papa!" she said reprovingly, stopping to admire a bed of floxemias. "Not to mention very gouty."

"Then was it perhaps . . . Truxton?"

"Truxton? Really, George, Bob Truxton was young enough to be . . . well, not precisely my son, unless I married at twelve, which I do not believe anyone has done since the Middle Ages, but he has barely been down from Oxford for a year!"

"Well, then, tell me who my rival is!" George implored.

"You," Miss Webster said calmly.

George, stunned, stopped dead in his tracks. "Me? But how . . . ? I mean . . ."

Miss Webster hoped she was not a prideful sort of female, but she did feel a slight twinge of irritation at George's obtusiveness.

"Well, consider, then, Lady Serena Ramplesham," she said, not unreasonably. "Only a fortnight ago, you came to me and asked my advice about the best way to offer for *her*." She turned toward George, her green eyes very large. "No female likes to be put into the position of feeling herself a second choice, George."

Lord Ventor bit his lip. "Well, dash it, Lizzie, a fortnight ago, I was a great fool! Mean to say, well, Lizzie, you know I'm not much in the petticoat line, but a fortnight ago, you and I . . . well, there had not been a great deal of princessing and hedge-taverning and Ben Sticking and adventuring about! What I mean to say is . . ." George paused, tugging at his hair in his search for words. "Thing of it is, she's a beauty, Lizzie! Can't help me if I was taken in by her looks and didn't see what she really is until Charlotte led her to it! Dashed bad thing, don't you know? Thing of it, think on, is that I never loved Serena! Didn't know what love was until . . . until . . ."

"Until what, George?" Miss Webster inquired mildly, turning to look at him from beneath the brim of her hat.

George shifted uneasily, made as if he would take her arm, failed in his courage to do so, and thrust his hands into the pockets of his breeches, frowning unhappily. "Thing of it is, Lizzie, made a damn cake of myself over Serena Ramplesham. Thought she was a good-lookin' sort of female, and that it was my duty to marry someone. Carry on the family name and all that! Dash it, Lizzie, it wasn't until the princess came along, and you came to my aid without so much as a why-should-I that I realized ... that I realized you were the only female in the world I should ever marry!"

"I am honored!" Miss Webster pronounced. "Are you asking me to marry you now, George?"

He coughed uncomfortably. "Well, as a matter of fact, I am!"

"Ah," Miss Webster said, as if that explained it all. "I see."

"Thought you might," George said. "Will you?"

"Marry you?" Elizabeth said thoughtfully. "I must think about that. It is very sudden, you know."

George stared after her. As if she had forgotten his existence, Miss Webster continued to stroll on down the path, stopping to talk to one of the undergardeners about the care and clipping of a boxwood hedge.

George was, not for the first time in his life, nonplussed. His experience of the female sex was not large, for he was not, as his late brother had been, greatly in the petticoat line. He was dimly aware that somewhere along the line, he had badly botched his proposal, both in his timing and in his delivery, but he could not quite see how Lady Serena Ramplesham figured into it.

Somewhere along the line, he understood, he had contrasted Miss Webster with that other lady, but now he failed to understand that he had not completely explained the shallowness and falsity of his attachment to that other lady to the complete satisfaction of Miss Webster. That his experiences in the past fortnight had taught him that his oldest friend Lizzie was not merely a friend but the everything of his life, he thought he had explained sufficiently to make her understand. What else, then, would she possibly demand of him? It did not occur to him that his proposal, coming so swiftly upon the heels of his rejection by Lady Serena, might make it appear to Miss Webster that she was merely second best, that somehow it had been brought home to him that he must marry, and lacking the hand of Lady Serena, hers was the most convenient to seek.

Since it was impossible to remonstrate with her while she was engaged in discussion with the undergardener, he merely shuffled about on the path, kicking stones out of his way and looking very ferociously indeed at that minion, until finally that young man caught his eye, and with a hurried tug at his forelock, found pressing needs in the privet hedge down by the south lawn.

Thus George was once again in a position to pursue Miss Webster, and he lost no time in doing so, catching up with her by the ornamental lake.

"Lizzie!" George called after her, gripping at her arm and making her turn about to face him. "You know me—have known me all my life! Know that I'm no hand with fancy words and flourishments!"

"Then say what is on your mind, George. I am perfectly willing to listen," Miss Webster replied, looking up into his eyes, a faint line between her brows, her fingers spinning at her parasol. If she felt a trifle irritated, there was no one who could blame her, for it must be recalled that she had dealt with a great deal from George's happenstance in the past two weeks, and no doubt expected to deal with a great deal more before the princess was finally restored to the hands of her hearty governess. "You know that I always listen to you, George," she added, a trifle more yielding.

"Lizzie, dash it, can't you see? Serena Ramplesham was all a moon-game for me! If it weren't for the princess, well, I probably would have married her, and lived the rest of my days to regret it! Particularly when you were right next door all my life! Yes, I was right next door to you—and fool that I was, I never recognized that my feelings toward you were more than just those of a friend, until it was almost too late! Lizzie, in the past fortnight I've come to realize that it's you I love!"

The hand which twisted the delicate ivory handle of the parasol about wavered slightly with this declaration, but, true to his own nature, George plunged heedlessly onward over the cliff.

"It only needed the contrast between your behavior and Lady Serena Ramplesham's for me to see which direction my heart lay in! If you could have only seen her, Lizzie, the tantrums, the hysterics, the jealousy with which she reacted when I appeared at her door, hoping for her help with the princess, you too would have known at once that she was not the helpmeet for me—indeed, for any good country man with a host of emergencies at hand! But you, Lizzie, you've been a capital sort of sport—you came right away, and helped me when I dared trust no one else. What I would have done without your help, I do not know!"

"My *help*," Miss Webster said wistfully, shaking her head. "Dearest George, if you only knew! I have been helping you since you were six years old and stranded in a pear tree in Squire Allway's orchard. I do not think a woman wants to be proposed to by a man who considers her a capital sort of sport, George! Somehow, you know, it is not very romantic at all! It sounds more as if you are seeking out a replacement for Mrs. Gurney!"

"Dammit, Lizzie, I'm trying to tell you that I love you!" George sputtered out.

Elizabeth peered up at him from beneath the brim of her hat. "You also said that you loved Serena Ramplesham—enough to marry *her*, and that not above two weeks ago, if I recall. George, I have always thought you were my friend, but never did I think *you*, of all persons, were of such an unsteady character. Not to mention fickle!"

"But it's you I love! I know that now!"

"I wish that were true, George, for my feelings toward you have ... have always been steady. Ever since I can recall," Miss Webster replied, her voice shaking with emotion. But she would not look at him, but rather looked away, across the greenish waters of the ornamental lake.

"Then you love me too, Lizzie—what could be simpler?" George asked plaintively.

"Believe me, I am happy to know that you love me, George," Elizabeth sighed, "but I cannot help but think that yours is only a *tendre* developed in light of recent affairs. Lady Serena has rejected you, and you must needs cast about for another wife, so what could be more simple than your choosing me? Oh, George, it is above all things unfair—how can you expect me to feel that you will not regret your decision in a week or a month or even a year, when someone better suited to your tastes comes along?"

"But you are suited to my tastes in every way, Lizzie!"

She shook her head. "I think not. If it were you, you would have known it before you paid your court to Serena Ramplesham!"

"Hang Serena Ramplesham!" George exclaimed, all *aux anges*. "Lizzie, it was at one of those interminable soiree crushes at my Aunt Augusta's. At the time, I had just received a lecture from my aunt concerning my duty to marry, and then *she* was thrown at my head! I had never had a chance to think about it, but that m'aunt and her mother had thrown her at me! I was besotted! I didn't know then what I know now! Lizzie, believe me, I do know this: I love you, and without you my life would be utterly miserable! You must believe me!"

"I *think* that I do, George," Elizabeth said slowly, turning to look at him, a faint smile crossing her features.

"Well, then," George demanded, "will you marry me?"

Elizabeth sighed. "Let us dispose of the princess first, George, then I think we may discuss it. Who knows but what we may both find our heads upon Traitor's Gate before too much longer?"

"Hang the princess!" George said, thoroughly irritated. "I wish I never had seen her!"

The result of this statement was rather more than George had expected. Elizabeth threw her arms about him and laid her head against his chest. "Oh, George, I was so afraid that it was quite the opposite!" she exclaimed.

George, while gratified by this sudden and unlikely demonstration of affection, was also a little puzzled, and as his arms reached out to reciprocate the gesture, he asked, puzzled, "Whatever do you mean, Lizzie?"

"I thought it was the *princess* for whom you had developed a *tendre*, and that you were simply . . . that I was once again your second best! Oh!" Elizabeth cried, much relieved.

"You were *never* second best! And certainly not with Charlotte!" George exclaimed indignantly, pushing Elizabeth away to arm's length to look at her upturned face. "Why, she's no more than a schoolgirl, let alone being one of the most trying, stubborn, hey-go-mad creatures I've ever run up against in my life! I only hope the man who chooses her for a wife has better sense than to let her have her full rein, or it's a merry chase she'll lead him, I can promise you that! What, me in love with Princess Charlotte? You must be mad!"

"Indeed, I must!" Elizabeth said, her voice

somewhere between a laugh and a sob as George embraced her firmly in his arms and kissed her with such passion that there could be no doubt at all left in her mind as to what the true state of his heart might be.

"Oh!" Elizabeth said breathlessly when he finally released her. "I never knew . . . that is, are you very sure this time, George?"

"I could be no more certain about anything than how much I love you, my dear!" George said, and demonstrated his affection again, and in such a forceful manner that Miss Webster's hat was knocked off her head, falling on its ribbons over her shoulders.

"Oh, George," she sighed, utterly contented at last in the surety that she knew where his heart lay.

"Now," George said when he released her again, but only a tiny bit, "I shall ask you again, and this time I want to hear nothing of Lady Serena or Princess Charlotte or indeed any other female save yourself. Will you marry me, Lizzie?"

"Oh, George—" Elizabeth started to say, but at that moment there was a discreet cough.

Dismayed, they both turned to see the august Fishbank standing in the path.

As guiltily as if they had been caught kissing on Bond Street at high noon, George and Elizabeth separated. She was blushing furiously, and George glowered at a man whom he had known all of his life. "Well, Fishbank, what is it?" he asked, his voice understandably surly.

Mr. Fishbank wrung his gloved hands. "Well, my lord, it is not at all what one is used to in a gentleman's household," he began, and was suddenly no longer the old and august butler who had served the Ventor family for forty-five years, but an old and somewhat confused man, as human as any of the footmen he had terrorized into dignity in the past half-century of service. "It is not *at all* what one is used to in a gentleman's household," he repeated, shifting from foot to foot.

"Well, what is it, dash it?" George asked.

"No doubt it's the militia come to arrest us all," Elizabeth said under her breath, putting hand to heart, which was thundering wildly.

"It's Mr. Trevor, sir." Fishbank's professional poise, upon which he prided himself highly, finally gave way, and he resembled something very much like a human being. "I always knew something like this would happen!" he exclaimed. "That one was never any good, even as a child, always hiding and sneaking up on people and doing heaven knows what sort of mischief!"

"My good man!" George exclaimed. "Get hold of yourself at once! Surely there is nothing even Mr. Trevor could have done to excite you thus!"

But Fishbank only shook his head, running

his gloved hands over his bald head and shaking in his shoes. From a pocket he produced a note, handing it to George with shaking hands.

"Mr. Trevor," he announced in a broken voice, "has eloped with Miss Prince, sir!"

16

After a luncheon of cheese and fruit, which he had eaten alone, Trevor, discovering the lady he knew as Miss Prince was still locked in her bedchamber as a result of the morning's disagreement with his cousin and Elizabeth Webster, besought to amuse himself alone in the billiards room.

Unfortunately, Trevor was one of those individuals who are both incapable of amusing themselves and at the same time, when left unattended for long periods of time, more than likely to prove the ancient axiom that idle hands are the devil's workshop.

As he sank billiard balls into the pockets of the table, he brooded, as was his wont, over the various and sundry vicissitudes that had befallen him in the past fortnight and again and again returned to the same conclusion—

that his misfortunes could be laid solely at the feet of his cousin George.

His reasons for this train of thought were Byzantine at best, but somehow evolved from the idea that George was in possession of title, estate, fortune, and Miss Webster, all of which somehow or other should rightfully have belonged to him. Although how this was supposed to have been achieved was not, even in Trevor's rather clouded mind, clear, but as more and more time passed and he was left with the attentions of neither his cousin nor Miss Webster, it worked into his mind that he was the victim, not of his own follies, but of ill-usage upon the part of his cousin and the woman he had (vaguely, and in his own time) thought to make his wife.

When he happened to lean upon his stick and glance out the window, affording him an excellent view of the figures of Lord Ventor and Miss Webster strolling in the gardens, very much in a *tête-à-tête*, it was the final humiliation. The idea that George had stolen a march upon him and reached the attentions of Elizabeth before he had had time and inclination to press his own suit made his martyrdom complete. A vast feeling of ill-usage swelled in his chest, he threw down his cue, reaching for the bell-pull that would summon Fishbank to pack his things in preparation for a hasty and indignant departure from Ventor Hall—and recollected at the last moment that he was literally without anywhere else to go until certain pressing obligations had been settled, or certain most ungentlemanly characters would, in lieu of ready blunt, exact payment by inflicting physical injury on his person.

It left him in a very bad situation indeed, he reflected, and bit on a nail as he rehearsed all of the most cutting remarks he would employ over the dinner table in order to wound those whose selfishness had so grievously deprived him of what he considered to be his rightful deserts.

He had just realized that any attempt to wound the sensibilities of the rather obtuse George would bear a resemblance to hitting the hide of an elephant with a volley of straight pins when there was a knock upon the door, and the lady he knew as Miss Prince thrust her head into the room, none the worse for the derangement of her tantrum that morning.

"Oh, pardon me!" she said, frowning slightly. "I had hoped to find Miss Webster here—I suppose you do not know what a terrible nodcock I made of myself this morning!"

For Trevor's devious mind, it was as if the gods had sent the answer to his prayers.

With a quick glance at the mirror to be certain that his cravat was arranged in perfect folds and that no ill-temper marred the physical perfection of his features, he whipped about, extending his hands toward the somewhat startled princess in a melodramatic manner.

"Ah, Miss Prince! I was just about to summon you!" he said.

"Ah?" Charlotte's eyes grew wider.

"Yes, my dear," Trevor continued, advancing upon her. "You must flee! All has been discovered! My cousin and Miss Webster are not the friends you believed them to be! Even now they are down in the garden plotting against you!"

Whatever Trevor's faults might have been, and they were numerous, somewhere along the line he had learned Dr. Johnson's axiom that if one were to announce to any party whatsoever that *all has been discovered*, one was bound to get a reaction. Several times in the past he had used this to his own gain, and this time was no exception, for the princess's reaction was precisely what he wished.

Her face grew pale, she pressed a hand to her bosom, and her blue eyes enlarged. "Papa," she said in trembling accents. "They have told Papa where I am and he means to find me!"

"Yes, yes, your papa is on his way, thanks to my cousin, and a rare taking the gentleman is in, I understand!" he assayed, and was rewarded with all the reaction he could have wished for.

Charlotte seemed to go weak in the knees, leaning haphazardly against the doorjamb, her bosom heaving in gasps, her eyes as wide as saucers. "H-how could they have d-done so?" she demanded, her voice quivering. "They ... they promised to restore me to m-my governess in Bath!"

Trevor, having discovered the information he sought, began to embroider upon it with diabolical designs. Sadly he shook his head. "It's all because you took me up in the phaeton this morning," he said. "They decided they could stand no more of your company, that you were a hindrance to them, and better restored to your father than left here to create more mischief!"

"No—it cannot be possible! They know how things stand between my father and me! I only want to go to Mrs. Campbell in Bath—it is all I have ever wanted! It is why I ran away from home!"

This scrap of further enlightenment made Trevor's brows rise slightly. Assisting runaway schoolgirls was something he definitely felt his cousin was far too staid to be doing, let alone involving Miss Webster in the game. For a moment he had a passing respect for this hitherto undiscovered facet of staid, rather dull George's character, but before he could give himself up to admiration, he recalled the circumstances, and regarded Miss Prince's comely face and figure with the admiration of an experienced womanizer. Resolve and revenge hardened his already ruthless character and he only nodded unhappily, sighing.

"You would think to look at the pair of them that butter wouldn't melt in their mouths," he suggested.

"I cannot! I *will* not go back to Papa! Not with things as they stand!" Miss Prince exclaimed, distraught, wringing her hands. "I must go to Mrs. Campbell in Bath! Good sir, you will help me!"

It was the invitation that the wolf had been waiting for the sheep to issue. It was all Trevor could do not to lick his chops. "But of course! Always at the service of a lady! If it's Bath you want to go to, Bath is where I shall convey you instantly. You have only to give the word!"

Charlotte's reaction was all that Trevor could have wished for. Impulsively she threw herself into his arms, proclaiming herself forever in his debt, and announcing that he was her hero.

"Tosh," Trevor said modestly, although his thin chest swelled with pride. "It is what any man would do for a damsel in distress! I know a certain quiet, discreet inn just outside of Bath, where we may be safe."

"Then let us go at once!" Charlotte announced.

Trevor was slightly taken aback. "Er, don't you want to pack your things?" he asked. "This thing requires planning, you know! And money," he added, recalling that his pockets were sadly to let. "I don't suppose you've got—"

Princess Charlotte, who had never worried about money in her entire royal life, merely shrugged. "Mrs. Campbell will restore to you all that you need! It is only a journey to Bath, after all, not to the other side of the moon! Quick! Order up your phaeton!"

Trevor shook his head. "I don't have a phaeton!" he announced. "Have to borrow George's!"

"Well, then do so! I shall pack my portmanteau and meet you down by the stables in a half-hour!" With those imperious words, Charlotte disappeared around the corner, leaving Trevor to sigh after her.

Clearly, this business of revenge and seduction was going to be more than he had bargained for. Harnessing his own—well, George's—team! It was outside of what a gentleman was used to doing!

Nonetheless, when he got his cozy little bird to the inn he habitually used outside Bath, he was certain it was all going to be worth it.

17

Two hours later, Elizabeth stood in the garden and with trembling hands broke the seal of the note Princess Charlotte had left behind.

"What does its say?" George asked, peering over her shoulder.

" 'Lord Ventor and Miss Webster,' " Elizabeth read in a tremulous voice:

Mr. Worthington has revealed all to me and I am going to Bath with him rather than stay here and await the return of Papa, whom I do not wish to see under the circumstances. I am very sorry that I have caused you so much pain, but only consider what Betrayal I must feel that you would so Callously turn me over to the one man who is the cause of all my unhappiness.

Adieu,
Charlotte

"Good God!" George exclaimed. "Fishbank! How came you by this?"

"One of the maids found it upon Miss Lizzie's pillow when she went to make up the bed," Fishbank said. "And a quarter-hour ago, the stables reported that Mr. Trevor had hitched up your phaeton himself and left. Oh, sir, I know Mr. Trevor and I know this can lead to no good! he has whisked that poor Miss Prince away from the Hall, and if I may speak frankly, sir, heaven only knows what deviltry he is up to this time!"

"George, you don't think that even Trevor—" Elizabeth started to say.

With a gesture, George silenced them both. "I know Trevor well enough to know he's up to his old mischief again!" he exclaimed.

"And you also know, if he succeeds, it's high treason," Elizabeth whispered in an undertone.

"Good God!" George exclaimed. Turning to Fishbank, he said, "I know that you will not say anything to the rest of the staff about this . . ."

Fishbank cleared his throat. "Mrs. Gurney used some rather severe threats with the house-maid who discovered the note, sir, but as far as that goes, I believe everyone can be, er, trusted, sir!"

"If I know Trevor, then I know precisely where he has taken Miss Prince—and my pha-eton!" George said, turning to walk up toward the house. "Fishbank, give the order to have the barouche made ready! Elizabeth, it would be best if you were to remain here—"

"Oh, no you don't!" Miss Webster exclaimed, her eyes flashing. "A very picture it would make if you were to drag her roy ... Miss Prince back here in one of her dungeons! Best I come along and talk sense into her! You know how persuasive Trevor can be when he's in one of his moods!"

"Aye, I'll persuade *him!*" George threatened darkly. "Trevor's gone too far this time!"

Lord Ventor and Miss Webster hurried toward the house, their thoughts in a world apart, for neither of them needed to speak the dreadful consequences that were on their minds.

They had just reached the stairs when the sound of an uncertain footman's voice protested from the doorway, "I say, sir, you can't come in here like that—"

"I can and I will!" exclaimed a voice with the faintest trace of a foreign accent. "Step aside, man, and let me through!"

As the pair upon the staircase turned, a tall man in the elaborate buff-and-green uniform of the Gotha Hussars strode across the stone floor. A shako was set upon his black curls, and his cape swirled about his dashing body, the dim light of late afternoon glittering off masses of gold braid, frogs, and epaulets. Beneath his heavy brows, a magnificent pair of dark eyes glittered as they took in the hall, and his long, aristocratic nose quivered indignantly above a sweeping black mustache as his highly polished cavalry boots jangled their spurs on the stone. The soldier was the very portrait of towering rage, and for a moment it crossed Miss Webster's mind that Napoleon had escaped again from Elba and invaded the country, and this was his henchman come to commandeer Ventor Hall for his occupying army.

George was descending the stairs, crossing the floor toward the man with a look of impatience upon his face. "See here, my good fellow, I don't know who you are or what you want, but I must tell you that—" he began.

The hussar was no taller than George, but beneath his commanding shako, with its plumes and leather medallion, he gave the appearance of having several inches upon the other man. He stared down his long nose at Lord Ventor for several seconds and then asked in his slight accent, "You are Lord Ventor, Viscount Ventor of Ventor Hall?"

"I am, but what the devil—" George started to say, when the hussar, with a high swing of a mighty glove, hauled back and deliberately smote the viscount across the face.

"Oh!" Elizabeth cried, picking up her skirts and running down the stairs toward them. "How dare you? you . . . you odious man!"

The hussar's heavy eyebrows rose to meet his shako. "*I* odious, ma'am?" he asked in surprise. "But I have only done what honor dictated! In my country, sir, I should have you drawn and quartered, you . . . you . . ." Before he could inflict further harm on George, who was standing as one stunned, with a hand pressed to his flaming cheek, a familiar voice broke in.

"Here, now, chappie, all's well when's said and done, but no need to land the toff a facer!"

As a well-known figure restrained the hussar from doing further damage to the viscount, Miss Webster exclaimed, "Ben Stick! But why . . . how . . . who is this man?"

It took some doing, but Ben Stick, resplendent in his spotted kerchief and pantaloons of shabby buckskin, managed to doff his low-crowned beaver slightly in Elizabeth's direction. "H'd'ew, ma'am?" he asked in a conversational tone. "That's it, governor, stow your manners an' doff yer hat, there's a lady present, prince or not!"

The hussar drew a deep breath and glared at the astonished George, who looked very much as if he wished to return the compliment with a facer of his own. "Ben, I know not how you found us, nor why you brought this man here, but I must say I think it damned sad of you to betray a friendship!"

"Friendship! Friendship! How dare you speak of friendship, you . . . you loose fish! You vile seducer!'' The hussar struggled in Ben's grasp without avail.

"Should I call for the magistrate, sir?" the footman asked, his eyes as wide as saucers, his mouth agape as he beheld the totally unexpected scene of his master being assaulted by an impressively uniformed foreigner being held in check by a cove, who, if his instincts were right, was on the sad side of the law.

"No constable coves here, my lad! Not while Ben Stick's about!" the highwayman commanded, still holding the struggling hussar with his arms tightly bound behind him. "That won't tip the dibs, mark my words!"

"No, no magistrates," George agreed, rubbing his jaw regretfully. "Ben, who is this fellow?"

"Who am I? Who am I? I am Prince Leopold of Saxe-Coburg-Gotha, sir, come to demand satisfaction from you for seducing away the woman I intend to make my wife!" announced the hussar. "And I intend to have you, sirrah, so name your weapons!"

"It is Prince Leopold!" Miss Webster exclaimed. "*Charlotte's* Prince Leopold!"

"But how . . .?" George asked, all at sea.

"I shall kill you! Like a dog!" the prince exclaimed passionately. "You are vile, sirrah! You do not see the daylight!"

"Your highness! That is quite enough!" announced a small, rather dowdy lady as she marched through the door clutching a reticule in one hand and a sensible-looking black umbrella in the other. "If you please, you will be good enough to act like a prince, sir! And you, Mr. Stick, will be good enough to unhand Prince Leopold!"

"And who, may I ask," George exclaimed, overcome, "are you?"

The little lady, dressed in a sensible traveling pelisse of Scotch merino, a plain bonnet placed over her iron-gray curls, peered at him from over her iron spectacles. "Why, I am Mrs. Alicia Campbell, and if I am correct, you must be Lord Ventor."

"Ventor! I spit upon your very name!" Prince Leopold shouted.

"The Princess Charlotte's governess!" Elizabeth exclaimed. "Oh, how very glad we are to see *you!*"

Mrs. Campbell, in the act of tapping Prince Leopold on the epaulet with her umbrella in the restraining sort of way she might have employed with a recalcitrant schoolboy, nodded. "Indeed, I am that Mrs. Campbell, and I fear that Lord Ventor, whom I perceive to be this gentleman here"—she gestured with the umbrella—"reached me too early to deliver the princess into my charge. So much like her father, I fear," she added.

"But when . . . how . . . ?"

"Very simple," Mrs. Campbell said with the

air of one instructing a slow student. "I returned from my holiday in the Lake District to find that my dear princess had left a message concerning her whereabouts at an inn called the Blood and Feather. As I had feared, her father's rather high-handed dismissal of all her ladies from Warwick House and her banishment to Cranbourne Lodge led her to do a very naughty thing indeed in running away." Mrs. Campbell shook her head, smiling at George. "But fortunately she found a knight in Lord Ventor, who shielded her from the very worst of her follies. I was just about to set out from Bath in search of my charge, to persuade her that she must return to Windsor, when his royal highness, who had somehow discovered her missing from Weymouth, where she was *supposed* to be, came looking for her at my house." Her blue eyes twinkled indulgently, and the prince bowed from the waist.

"If anyone has as much as harmed a hair on her head, I shall *kill* him," he threatened, looking at George.

"Well, at the Blood and Feather, a most interesting place indeed, I may add—"

"A hellhole for thieves and murderers! Not fit for her to place one tiny toe in!" The prince glowered.

"Well, gov, it may not be much to you, but to some of us, we call it *home*," Ben Stick put in defensively.

Like a fairy with a magic wand, Mrs. Campbell waved her umbrella in the air, and the party fell silent. "As I was saying," she continued with an air of mild reproof in her voice, "the prince and I repaired to the Blood and Feather, where Mr. Stick was, er . . . prevailed upon to lead us to Ventor Hall."

"Very likely the bloody prince would have eaten my brains for breakfast iffen I hadn't," Ben grumbled. "Sorry I tipped yer dubbs, but you do see how it was, don't you, George old man?"

George could only nod.

"Of course, you were threatened. And you knew the princess was the princess, poor Ben," Elizabeth said sympathetically.

"I can promise you that she was in no way harmed."

"Indeed, Lord Ventor did everything he could to protect her! I have chaperoned her every move since George sent for me!"

"It was the folly of a moment, you see, when I saw her taking the Bristol coach," George agreed.

"Anyway, iffen you was to ask me, there's not a thing on the face of this earth that would induce his lordship to have a flier at her royal highness. At it tooth and nail all the while they were, him tryin' to keep her in line and her tryin' to act the hoyden. Why—"

"I assure you there is nothing that would

persuade me to entertain amorous attentions toward that hellion, heiress apparent of England or not!" George said bitterly, glaring at Prince Leopold.

"Sir, you speak of the woman I love!" the prince said, and it appeared as if they would have flown at each other's throats at that very moment, had the footman not announced:

"Miss Prince, my lord!"

All things forgotten in the moment, everyone turned to watch as Charlotte, somewhat rumpled in her borrowed habit, but none the worse for wear, tripped through the front door, bearing her driving whip and stripping off her gloves. She looked about the company for a stunned moment, taking it all in, and then exclaimed, "Leopold!" in such tones of endearment that there could be no mistaking the affection in which that person was held by her royal highness.

"My dearest Charlotte!" the prince replied, royal dignity forgotten for the moment as the handsome hussar swept the princess up into a powerful embrace.

"The phaeton has returned, my lord, and the barouche is prepared," Fishbank said as he staggered through the door, his jaw dropping in bewilderment as he watched the embrace of this couple.

"Your royal highness," Miss Webster finally inquired, "where is Mr. Worthington?"

Princess Charlotte looked completely blank for a moment. "Oh, *him*," she said, loath to release the grasp of her beloved. "I believe I left him on the road to Hand Cross. He did not believe that I could drive to an inch, you see."

Elizabeth was never certain if the princess dropped a wink or not, for at that moment Prince Leopold seized her wrist and drew himself up to his full height. "With your leave, Lord Ventor, is there a place where her royal highness and I might have a private word?"

Wordlessly George gestured toward the Gold Salon. Fishbank, who knew what was worthy of the Hall, approached with stately tread. "If your highnesses will be good enough to follow me," he suggested, leading the way, "I will have Madeira and biscuits sent in directly."

He gave an imperious gesture at the gasping footman and led the boy away, but as he trod down the passageway, he could be seen shaking his head sadly.

"I think that I should like a glass of Madeira myself," said Mrs. Campbell, who acted as if her erstwhile charge's behavior were the normal peccadilloes of any well-brought-up young lady. "And I think also that I should like to hear all that has transpired. The Regent, you know, much repents of his hasty behavior, and will want to hear all that has befallen his daughter—or all that I shall choose to tell him."

"Perhaps the library," Elizabeth suggested,

with a wondering look at George as the remainder of the entourage trooped into that room.

It was fully an hour before the romantic royals joined them in that room. The princess was looking very subdued, but also happy as Prince Leopold linked his arm into hers and announced, "Her royal highness has very graciously consented to become my wife! A toast!"

"To the firm resolve that there will be no further royal escapades of this sort to trouble Miss Webster and Lord Ventor," the princess suggested, smiling as George poured another glass of Madeira all around.

"I should thoroughly hope not!" George said as he handed the princess her glass. "As for me, I have had enough adventure to last me a lifetime in the past fortnight!" He put Elizabeth's hand into the crook of his arm and she looked up at him with a smile.

"And you must all attend our wedding!" the princess said as glasses were raised to her.

"Indeed," agreed the prince, his hussar mustache bristling.

"It is to be hoped that you will come," Mrs. Campbell said, placing her glass on the table and shaking out her skirts as she rose, consulting the turnip watch on her bosom. "But now I think we must take our leave! There is a very anxious parent awaiting our return to Bath!"

"Only one other thing remains," the princess said, taking George and Elizabeth's hands in her own. "To thank you both very much—it was an adventure and a lesson! A lesson from which I learned a great deal!"

Elizabeth murmured all that was proper, and the prince shook their hands heartily, promising that if ever they should need anything, they were to call upon him at once. "For I owe you my happiness!" he exclaimed gruffly.

"Oh!" said Charlotte, nearly out the door, escorted by the prince as if he feared to lose her again. "And one other thing!"

She placed something in Ben Stick's hand and whispered in his ear. Rapturously he knelt and she tapped him on either shoulder with two fingers of her right hand. "Arise," she said majestically, "Sir Benjamin Stick, Knight."

"Cor," Ben Stick said, at a loss for words. He looked about the room. "She made me a knight!"

The prince and princess, together with Mrs. Campbell, were gone, leaving nothing behind them but the vague essence of Mrs. Campbell's rosewater in the air.

"If I had not lived through it," Elizabeth said, sinking exhausted into a chair, "I would not have believed it."

"She made me a knight," Ben Stick repeated wonderingly, fingering a guinea the princess had pressed into his hand. He frowned thoughtfully. "Trouble is, how am I to go back to the

High Toby a knight? Somehow it just don't look right, iffen you know what I mean."

"Then it is honest employment you need," George informed him with a grin. "A knighthood is all very well, but it won't pay for your pint. How would you like to stay here and be my groom . . . er, Sir Ben?"

Ben's face lit up. "Now, that I would like, George . . . er, my lord, I guess it would be now, iffen the wages were right, an' no more stray princesses, mind!"

"I can promise you both!" George agreed with a laugh. "And your first duty will be to take the phaeton and the barouche back to the stables and see to the horses!"

"No," Elizabeth said, twining her arm into George's. "Your first duty will be to see that no one disturbs us!"

Enlightenment dawned on Sir Benjamin Stick, and as he closed the door upon the embracing couple, he loftily informed Fishbank that the sound of wedding bells would be heard twice within the kingdom, mark his words.

About the Author

CAROLINE BROOKS is a practicing gerentologist who resides in Rising Sun, Maryland, with her husband and three children. Her interest in the Regency period was sparked when she purchased an old diary from that era in a Charing Cross bookstall during a visit to London in her student days.